"Hermits are vastly underrated."

Rainie rolled out of bed and walked to her closet. "If word ever gets out, none of you will be left alone."

Lucas sobered. "I wish you didn't think of me as a hermit. It sounds too antisocial."

"Well, aren't you? Otherwise why would you have tried so hard to get rid of me?"

He swung his legs over the edge of the bed and started dressing. "Maybe because you were being a pest."

"There's no need for you to pretend to be brusque." She zipped her jeans and went to a drawer to get a bra. "I can see right through you."

He grinned. "It's a shame you can't go around dressed like that all the time. I'm not sure I could ever argue with you."

"That's good to know. The next time you're being impossible, I'll know what to do." She glanced over at him and smiled mischievously. "Let's hope we aren't in public at the time."

Lynda and Dan Trent have been coauthors for almost as long as they've been married. They met, fell instantly in love, married and drifted into a writing partnership that has produced dozens of books praised by readers and critics alike. The phenomenal success of their collaboration extends to their personal life as well, where they have succeeded in blending two families into one. The Trents now live with their four children in East Texas, where they are both active in community theater.

Books by Lynda Trent

HARLEQUIN SUPERROMANCE
121–WINTER ROSES
348–THE GIFT OF SUMMER

Don't miss any of our special offers. Write to us at the following address for information on our newest releases.

Harlequin Reader Service
901 Fuhrmann Blvd., P.O. Box 1397, Buffalo, NY 14240
Canadian address: P.O. Box 603,
Fort Erie, Ont. L2A 5X3

Another Rainbow

LYNDA TRENT

Harlequin Books

TORONTO • NEW YORK • LONDON
AMSTERDAM • PARIS • SYDNEY • HAMBURG
STOCKHOLM • ATHENS • TOKYO • MILAN

Published March 1990

ISBN 0-373-25391-5

Printed in U.S.A.

1

"WILL SHE BE all right?" Rainie asked as the veterinarian ran his hand down the horse's knobby front legs. "What do you think?"

He paused before shaking his head. "You've let yourself in for a big one this time. These horses are more dead than alive."

"I know. That's why I bought them. Old man Fredricks ought to be fastened in a pen with no dry place to stand and nothing to eat or drink. Damn! I'm so mad I could cry." She pushed herself to her feet and shoved her palms into her jeans' pockets. "Is Tom going to arrest him?" she demanded.

"He already has, but Fredricks is out on bail."

Rainie paced to the side of the stall and rested her forearm on the rough plank. "Can you save them?"

Bob Pollard rose and looked over the six horses. "I think so. Most of them are young in spite of the way they look. If their health isn't broken by all the deprivation, I think they'll come around. Except for that old sorrel—she's way past her prime. I believe you'll lose her. And I'll be surprised if the colt over there isn't stunted. He's pretty active, but I'm not sure he's been fed enough for his bones to form right."

She went to the fidgety young animal and stroked his lackluster coat. "Bob, I could shoot Fredricks for doing this! All these lovely, gentle horses!"

"The whole town is up in arms over it. Tom said a TV film crew was there when he made the arrest. Once pictures of that hellhole are aired, this incident won't be swept under the rug."

"It had better not be." She patted the colt's bony hip.

"It's just a good thing you noticed what was going on. With his barn and horse lot back from the road the way they are, how'd you happen to see them?"

"I was exercising India," she said with a nod toward a sleek black gelding in another stall. "As we passed Fredricks's place, India nickered, and one of these horses answered him. I didn't know Fredricks kept any animals at all, so out of curiosity I went back there and looked. Bob, it nearly made me sick to my stomach."

"Knowing Fredricks, it's a wonder he didn't shoot you. The mountain people in this part of Tennessee don't care much for uninvited people coming onto their property. You've lived here long enough to know that."

"Sometimes it's for reasons like this," she said, gesturing toward the malnourished animals. "There's no telling how many horses and cows that monster has let starve over the years! There were two cows and nine horses jammed into that mud hole, and these six are the only ones that didn't have to be destroyed on the spot!"

"I know. It turned my stomach, too."

Rainie watched one of the mares, who was heavy with foal, walk stiff-legged to the water trough. "I guess I always go off the deep end," she said. "At least I do when it's a matter of something being downtrodden. Animal or people, it's all the same."

Her dark blue eyes narrowed with remembered anger. "Fredericks came running out, yelling at me to get off his land, and I told him I wanted to buy all his livestock. I was afraid if I didn't offer to buy them, he would hide them before I could get the sheriff out there. I convinced him I had to go home and get my horse trailer, but when I came back, Tom and his deputies were with me. And the TV crew."

"How'd you manage to get the television station to respond so quickly? They're forty miles from here."

She shrugged. "They were doing a local interest feature on Essie Fay Emerson for being this county's oldest resident and were interviewing Tom—he's her great-grandson, you know—when I got to his office."

"That was a stroke of luck." Bob smiled. "But then, you're the luckiest person I ever met." He reached in his bag and pulled out a syringe.

"I guess you could say I'm lucky," she admitted. "At least I have been for the past several years. Being in the right place at the right time and taking advantage of opportunities that have come along has brought about a lot of changes in my life. Like my buying a horse farm. It was one of those spur-of-the-moment decisions, I guess you'd say. I was passing through and just fell in love with it. I was recently divorced, and I had no ties and a healthy financial settlement. When I saw this place was for sale, I bought it and moved in."

"Just like that?"

"Just like that." She brushed her dark, shoulder-length hair out of her face, and the corners of her mouth tilted up in the hint of a smile at the memory of her impulsive move. "My ex-husband told me I was crazy to even consider it. I think that's what convinced me. Generally speaking, Harry has always told me to do exactly the opposite of what I want to do."

"Well, from what I've seen, it seems to have been a good decision for you."

"I'm pretty content here. Lupine is small and picturesque and the people are friendly—at least they became friendly once they saw how eager I was to fit in. I love the serenity here in the mountains. I'd had it with city life, and especially with Louisville. Everything there reminded me of Harry."

Bob gave vitamin injections to all the horses, then as he compassionately patted the old sorrel mare, he noticed Rainie was staring off into the distance. "Marla says she thinks you must get lonely living by yourself out here."

"Sometimes. But town is only ten minutes by car and half an hour by horse. Or I can go down the mountain to Roan Oak, which isn't much farther. And Marla comes out to visit several times a week, or I go to her place." She gave Bob a sideways glance and teasingly commented, "Before long I won't have to drive so far to see her."

He grinned. He and Marla were engaged to be married within the month, and his farm bordered Rainie's. "Neither will I."

"You two look so happy together. I couldn't picture you with anyone else."

"Maybe you ought to consider remarrying. You'd be less lonely."

"Right after the divorce I was determined never to marry again. But lately, I have to admit it has crossed my mind, though I'd never go back to suburban life and schedules and races up the corporate ladder. I've had my fill of that."

"Then marry someone in Lupine," Bob suggested. "There are no suburbs or corporations here. Hardly any schedules, for that matter."

"There also aren't any eligible men."

"Tom Hanford is still single."

She smiled and shook her head. "You know Tom and I are just friends. Besides, Eva Jean Massey would scalp anyone who took a second look at him."

"True. I was just using him as an example."

"Besides, living alone has its advantages. If I want to read or make brownies at three in the morning, I don't disturb anyone. Or if I want to bring a saddle in and oil it while I watch TV, nobody tells me it's not the thing to do. If I have a sick horse, I can stay down here in the barn all night and not worry that someone is waiting up for me."

"You make it sound ideal."

Rainie smiled as though it were, but there were times when she was so lonely she cried, and there were nights when even Harry's arms about her would have felt good. She tried to keep such thoughts from her mind, and she certainly never admitted them to anyone else.

Bob gathered his things together, but before leaving, he extracted another large bottle of medicine from his bag. "Like I said, I think we're going to lose that old red mare, but give her a dose of this morning and night just like you do the others. Maybe she'll surprise us. Keep their hooves dry, especially that bay with the star face. His are in particularly bad shape and we don't want him to go down."

"Whatever you think is best."

"You can leave the back gate open so they can get out into the pen and get some sunshine, but keep them out of the pastures until they get their strength up, and fasten them in the barn if it rains. They don't have any resources right now to fight off infection."

"I understand." She walked Bob back to the battered truck he used to make his rounds. "I hope that mare doesn't go into labor while you're on your honeymoon."

"I don't think she's that far along. But as skinny as she is, it's hard to tell. I'm afraid the foal may be stillborn. Nature has a way of protecting its babies from devils like Fredricks. But offhand, I'd say she won't need me for another month or so."

He got in the truck and Rainie slammed the door with a clang. "Thanks for coming out, Bob. Between us, we'll pull them through. Even the red mare and the colt, when it comes."

"Optimism is good medicine," he said and waved as he drove away.

Rainie walked back into the dimly lit barn. Smells of hay and leather and horseflesh greeted her, and she inhaled deeply of the familiar scents. Her childhood on a ranch in Texas had given her a firm base on which to build what had always seemed to be an impossible dream. In her childhood fantasies it wasn't a pot of gold at the end of the rainbow, but rather a horse.

Her fondest daydreams were of her on a ranch full of horses, with a husband on whom she could lavish all her pent-up love and who would return that love measure for measure.

At one time she had thought Harry would be that man, but she soon found out Harry was really married to his job and to political maneuvering that would reap raises and promotions. Rainie had never been able to settle for a nice house and only crumbs of affection.

For a long time she had been convinced that the fault lay in herself. Harry had said she was too needy, too smothering, too demanding. Finally, after eight years of marriage, Rainie realized it wasn't smothering to want a kind word, and it wasn't too demanding of her to expect sex more frequently than once every other month. She did have to own the accusation of being emotionally needy, however. She needed, and was willing to give far more affection than Harry Dillard was able to give or willing to receive. Thus she had obtained a divorce, then armed with her maiden name and several thousand dollars from the settlement, Rainie Sheenan had set out to make a new life for herself.

The discovery of the small horse ranch had been a miracle, in her opinion, because she'd spotted it while gazing at a rainbow that seemed to point the way to it. She had fallen in love with the rustic house and barn and had bought it on the spot. Only one element was missing—the loving husband. So she had dubbed her place the "Rainbow Ranch" and had had that logo printed on her stationery and emblazoned on the arch above her gate. Because people generally minded their own business in the Tennessee mountains, no one ever asked why she had chosen such a fanciful name.

As she returned to the large stall that was usually reserved for grooming or for the confinement of brood mares, the six scrawny horses warily looked at her, and her heart again went out to them. They were still frightened, and she knew they would have tried to escape if they had had the energy. But she was confident that they would become accustomed to her before they regained their strength. She had a knack for building a rapport with animals in her care, even ones such as these which had been so abused. Talking softly and gently touching them, Rainie led them to the back wall and released the bolt on the door that opened onto the pen. Outside, the spring grass was lush. Slowly the horses followed the instinctively curious buckskin colt out into the sunlight.

In no time at all they began grazing, their square teeth ripping at the grass as if they could never get enough. Bob had cautioned her not to leave them on the grass for more than a couple of hours the first day, though she was already well aware that because of their deprivation, they might founder if allowed to eat without restraint.

Two hours would give her time to exercise India, her favorite saddle horse. Other animals had come and gone, but in the two years she had lived in Lupine, Rainie had always kept India for herself.

After saddling the black horse with the Western saddle she used for pleasure riding, she swung up onto his back. She disliked the pancake-flat-English saddles that were required for horse shows and only rode with one often enough to maintain her proficiency.

Her ride this day, however, wasn't solely for pleasure. Horse sales were up, so she was considering an expansion in her operations to include raising quarter horses, as well as saddle horses. With her interest in bluegrass horse racing, she had even considered at one time raising Thoroughbreds, but had decided against it because of the enormous overhead costs for the additional facilities and a staff of grooms and jockeys.

Rainie wanted to keep her operation small enough so she could handle it herself with only the two hired men from Lupine. Otherwise it sounded too much like big business and too reminiscent of Harry. She was in no danger of ever becoming rich, but she made enough to live comfortably and without worry. With her increase in livestock, however, she would need more land.

Her ranch was bounded on the front by a road and by Bob Pollard's land on one side and a farm on the other. Neither of her neighbors were interested in selling their land, and the acres across the road weren't suitable for grazing. That left only the land behind her ranch.

When she had first moved to Lupine, Rainie had wanted to buy that land, as well. It appeared to lay in a series of broad, lush natural meadows divided by fingers of the forest. Most of its acres crested the top of the low mountain and as a result these meadows would have been better suited to her horses than was her own ranch, which lay on the mountain's gentle slope.

When she had inquired around town, everyone had been vague about who owned the land, but all were positive it wasn't for sale. After some investigation she'd learned it was owned by a corporation, and she hadn't pursued it further. Harry had convinced her long before that dealing with big business was a pain, at best. However her curiosity about that land had not been squelched entirely.

She rode to the gate in the back fence of her property and sat for a minute, trying to decide whether she should risk trespassing for a closer look. Quickly reviewing the pros and cons, she concluded the odds were small that she'd get caught, and besides her interest was entirely harmless. Dismounting she began to wrestle with the wire loop that fastened the gate to the adjoining fence post.

As she struggled to get the gate open, it occurred to her that the very existence of a gate indicated that the two lands had at some time been owned by one individual, or that the relationship between the two property owners had been congenial.

Finally she succeeded in getting the gate open, but had second thoughts about trespassing. As she stared at the opening, contemplating how she would feel about someone taking such liberties with her property, she caught a flash of tan in her peripheral vision. By the time she realized the buckskin colt had escaped the pen and had followed her, he was darting past her through the gate.

"Damn!" she blurted out. "Whoa!" But the colt's spindly legs quickly took it up the narrow trail and out of sight around the first bend. She could hardly believe he was able to run and figured he wouldn't be too hard to find as he would surely tire quickly. After leading her horse through, Rainie closed the gate behind her and began looking for the colt, miffed that he had gotten out, but pleased for the legitimate excuse to look over the place.

The land gently sloped upward with banks of wild hydrangea and rosebay and flame azaleas of all colors. Springtime in the Smoky Mountains was like a trip to paradise. The way was relatively clear, as if there might once have been a wagon road through the woods. As Rainie rode along at an easy gait, scanning the openings in the vegetation for any sign of the colt, she speculated on who the forgotten people were who had lived here and used this path, and she wondered whether they had let the wild honeysuckle and berry vines grow so close to the path, or whether nature had done so in their absence.

Up ahead, the grass to the left of the path appeared to have been recently trampled, so she veered off in that direction. She figured it wasn't far to the fence line leading up the mountain and that the colt would likely follow the fence.

India proudly arched his neck and picked his way over the rock-strewn ground, as if he were humoring his mistress's latest quirk. India's demeanor was one of the reasons Rainie loved him so. He was regal and aristocratic, and always gave the impression that he was obeying simply to be gracious. She admired India's cool collectedness and decided to give him his head, thinking he might lead her to the errant colt.

As she had expected, the meadows here were natural ones, expansive enough to provide pastures for grazing, and the large trees would serve well as windbreaks against summer storms and winter snows. Also she discovered there were two separate streams, both of which ran clear and pure, and deep enough not to go dry in the summer. At the summit, India stopped and looked about as if he, too, were baffled as to the colt's whereabouts.

The view Rainie was afforded from this vantage point was indeed spectacular. Mountains tumbled in a blue haze as far as she could see, with gauzy green valleys below, and she spotted a silver ribbon of river that she knew to be the one that flowed through Lupine.

"What a perfect place to build a house," she said to her horse. "Look at this view!" She had grown accustomed to talking to her animals, and thought nothing of it. "I guess it would be rough in the winter, though," she admitted. India looked as if he couldn't care less.

"But it's perfect for horses. I could put the barn there where the trees would shelter it from the wind. In the winter I'd have to drive up here to feed, but my truck would make it once the pathway was widened into a road."

In the distance she heard a bobwhite call plaintively for his mate, and after a while came the single-noted answer. Spring was all around her, bursting and gurgling with life. This was her favorite season.

India restlessly tossed his head and his bit tinkled. "I know. I haven't forgotten the colt," Rainie responded. She pressed the reins against his neck and the horse obediently followed her command and headed down through the trees they had missed on the climb up. In no time she was again on the overgrown path.

She let India pick his way down the weed-choked road at his own pace as she peered about looking for some sign of the colt. Soon the thick woods closed around her, and Rainie felt the damp cool of the deep shade. Off to her right she heard the splash and tumble of a stream and wondered if the one on her land was a part of this one. If so, the water here would be good. Hers never ran dry in the summer, and she had assumed it was spring fed.

India stepped daintily into a clearing and Rainie hastily drew him to a halt. Blinking to be sure her eyes weren't playing tricks on her, she stared straight ahead at the buckskin colt grazing in front of a log cabin. But her biggest surprise was the tall, good-looking man who was standing on the porch glaring at her.

"Who are you?" he boomed.

"Rain . . . Rainie Sheenan," she managed to stammer, startled by his thunderous voice.

"What are you doing on my land?" He stepped out of the porch's shadows, looking even more authoritarian than before, and took a position at the rail. His black wavy hair, so long it touched his shoulders, glistened in the sunlight. His full beard, also black, was neatly trimmed close to his tanned face. Rainie was too far from him to make out the color of his eyes, but she had no doubt they were riveting her with a piercing stare. "Well?" he demanded.

"My horse, there," she said, pointing to the colt. "When I opened the gate back down the way, he darted through, and I had to find him."

"This is my land. Why were you opening my gate?" He eyed her as if she were a known criminal.

"Your land?" She dismounted with a length of rope in hand and easily moved toward the colt, hoping he wouldn't bolt. "Then we must be neighbors."

"I haven't got any neighbors." He leaned on the rail as if to drive home the point he was making. "Neighbors visit each other. I don't want any visitors."

Fortunately the colt had quickly tired himself, and made no protest when she slipped the noose around his neck. By now some of Rainie's initial fear was dissipating, and curiosity about this ruggedly handsome man was taking its place. "I've lived on the adjoining land for the past two years. Why have I never seen you? How could you get to Lupine without crossing my land?"

"I don't go to Lupine. When I need to go to town, I go to Roan Oak."

As the colt moved closer to the porch, Rainie followed. The man was not holding a gun, and other than the gruffness in his voice, which he seemed to be forcing, he didn't appear to be dangerous. "Are you all by yourself here? No family or anything?" From this closer perspective, she could see his eyes were brown—the reddish brown of pine bark. No, this man wasn't dangerous, but he was angry.

"That's right. I prefer it that way."

She glanced around. A dirt-clotted Jeep was parked next to some rusty farming equipment under a shed. In the side yard near the porch was a well and beyond that a narrow dirt road that led off in the general direction of Roan Oak. No electric lines crossed the clearing. "You don't have electricity?"

"I don't need it. Now if you'll just be on your way, Miss..."

She could still feel her pulse in her throat. "You can call me Rainie. Everybody does. Sheenan is my parents' name—and mine, too, for a while, of course—and then it was Dillard. Rainie Dillard. I hated that. But now I'm divorced and it's Sheenan again, but after it not being Sheenan for so long a time, I'm not sure it's really me anymore, so just call me Rainie."

He blinked. "What?"

"I said just call me Rainie." She wondered if he was hard of hearing, then with her courage rising, she smiled to put herself and him more at ease.

"Whoever you are, get the—"

"Actually I'm glad I ran into you," she interrupted. "It will save me trying to track you down. I'd like to buy your land, Mr. ..." She paused for him to supply his name.

He frowned at her and made no move to answer.

"What's your name?"

"My name?"

"Yes, of course. What do people call you?" She spoke slowly and distinctly in case his hearing wasn't quite up to par.

"Why do you want to know?"

She gave him an exasperated look. "We're trying to talk business here. I want to make you an offer on this land, and I need to know your name."

"My land isn't for sale." He scowled more fiercely and added, "Get out of here!"

"Now I'm not interested in haggling," she said as she took note of the way his muscled chest and and shoulders strained against the cloth of his red flannel shirt when he grew tense. His long legs were encased in close-fitting, faded jeans that looked soft from countless washings. To her surprise, she realized her thoughts had centered on his thighs, rather than on some innocuous question such as whether he washed those jeans at a washateria in Roan Oak or whether he beat them on a rock in the stream. Forcing herself back to the business at hand, she firmly stated, "I'm willing to pay you a fair price, but no more than that."

"Look, crazy lady, I'll overlook your trespassing this time, but don't come up here again. I want my privacy."

She could see the loneliness in his eyes. She was sure of it. And it was abundantly clear that he didn't want to discuss selling his land. "Do you like to read?"

He blinked again as if the route of the conversation eluded him. "Read? What?"

At once she was embarrassed for him; he didn't know how to read. A lot of people couldn't read, or they read so poorly it was a chore for them to struggle through words. Compassionately she said, "If you'd like, I could help you learn to read."

In an exasperated gesture, he shoved his fingers through his thick, black hair. "I can already read, damn it. What's that got to do with anything?"

"You look lonely. I thought maybe if I loaned you some books . . ."

"Now look! I'm not lonely, I'm alone. I want it that way. As for you loaning me some books, you can just . . ."

"I've embarrassed you, haven't I?" she commiserated. "I never meant to do that. Will you forgive me?"

"Look here, lady," he began with strained patience, "I—"

"Rainie," she prompted. "Remember?"

"I'm not likely to forget. Just don't explain it again."

She smiled at him and a dimple appeared on the right side of her chin. "What's your name?"

He paused as if he were reluctant to tell her. "Lucas Dalton," he said at last.

"What an interesting name! Sounds like you're somebody famous."

Lucas jerked his head around, an unasked question in his eyes.

"What I mean is, are you any kin to the infamous Dalton gang?"

"If I am, my father never admitted it." He was staring at her as if he couldn't decide what to make of her.

"I don't think they came from around here. Do you? Come from around here, I mean?"

His dark eyes swept her face as if he had expected some other response. "Is that all my name means to you? Just a reference to a band of long-dead outlaws?"

"I didn't mean to offend you. They may have been rather nice, personally. After all, how do we know?"

He seemed to relax a bit. "Yes, I'm from here. My family has owned this mountaintop since it was first settled."

"And that's why you don't want to sell it. I can understand that." Her face looked soft and crestfallen. "I guess I'd feel the same way. I don't hold it against you."

"That's a relief," he said wryly.

"Were you afraid I might?" she asked, missing his irony altogether. "How sweet. I never meant to worry you. And now you're looking lonely again."

"I'm looking as if I'm about to throw you off the mountain," he corrected.

Her lightning-quick smile returned. "You have a sense of humor! Listen, Lucas—I hope you don't mind if I call you Lucas, but 'Mr.' is so formal and 'Dalton' is rather formidable—I can see you really want to be friendly, but you're just shy. So here's what I'm going to do," she began as she mounted her horse and drew the colt closer to her. "I'm going to leave now, but I'll be back tomorrow with those books I promised you. No, don't thank me. I'll bring a whole assortment so you can choose what kind you like best, and if you have a bit of trouble reading, why, I'll be more than happy to help you with it." She pressed her heels against India's sides causing him to leap forward in a quick trot. Over her shoulder she called back, "I'll bring a picnic lunch, too."

She saw him step forward, holding up his hand as if in dispute, or was it meant to be a wave? Rainie waved back as India trotted into the forest with the new colt in tow.

A hermit! A real, live hermit living practically on her back fence! And he was young and tall and sexy—everything a person could hope to find in such a neighbor. Maybe the Lupine valley wasn't devoid of eligible men, after all.

2

"YOU'VE GOT SOME good-looking horses there," the sheriff said as he leaned on the fence. "Your stock's improving."

Startled, Rainie jumped and as she peered around the shaggy rump of one of her newly acquired horses, she smiled at the man's obvious jest. "I didn't hear you drive up." She'd been totally absorbed in her anticipation of seeing her reclusive neighbor again.

"Those watchdogs of yours are worse than worthless," he continued to tease. "I had to step over them to get on your porch. Nearly woke them up. When you didn't answer the door, I assumed you'd be out here."

"You're right. They aren't much good as watchdogs," she conceded with a grin as she went back to brushing the painfully thin horse. "But they're sweet."

"You know, I never would have guessed anyone would want these animals. I've seen people adopt small animals before, but these horses take the cake."

"I guess I was impulsive. Bob says he doesn't think they'll all pull through. But I couldn't bear the thought of having them destroyed, if there was any chance of saving them."

Tom Hanford let himself through the gate and crossed to the tethered bay. "Yeah, I'm the same way. This could have been a fine horse, if he'd had good treatment."

Rainie looked up at the sheriff in anticipation. "I hope you're out here to tell me you found some way of locking up old man Fredricks and throwing away the key."

"No, afraid not. I wish I could. One of his daughters from over in Memphis bailed him out. I reckon the judge will give him a stiff fine, especially since we got so many calls after the story hit the news. But knowing Fredericks, the threat of being caught again won't stop him from doing something like this another time."

She turned to face him. "Are you serious?"

"Yep. So I've been out to his place to have a talk with him. You know I drive by there every time I go to see Eva Jean."

Rainie nodded. Tom's courtship of Eva Jean was the longest in Lupine's history, according to local gossip.

"Well, I let him know, off the record so to speak, that he and I were going to be real close friends, and that he could count on me dropping by at odd times just to pass the time of day, friendly like. I also let him know that if I ever had a hint that he was mistreating anything from a goldfish to an elephant, I would arrest him again."

"What did he say to that?"

Tom chuckled, his round belly jiggling. "He sputtered and hemmed and hawed and finally allowed as how it would be okay. Wasn't much else he could do as long as I'm not in uniform and keep it looking like a neighborly call."

Rainie smiled in appreciation. Sometimes Sheriff Hanford's frequent neighborly visits were a nuisance, but this would serve a useful purpose. "Want a cup of coffee, Tom? I've got some brewing in the kitchen."

"No, thanks. Maybe next time. I told Eva Jean I'd pick her up at the beauty shop around noon and take her out for lunch. It's getting near that time now."

"Is it?" Rainie squinted up at the sun. "I had no idea it was that late."

"You ought to wear a watch."

"Not me. That's part of my new image. I threw away my watch when I left the city. I barely even read a calendar."

The sheriff shook his head. "I sure never met up with any-one the likes of you. Say, did that old yellow cat of yours ever have kittens?"

"She sure did. Want one?"

"Not me, but Eva Jean does. Her old cat ran away the other day. The one she was so fond of." He lowered his voice as if they might be overheard. "I didn't say so to her, but I expect he went off to die. Cats will do that, you know, and he was real old."

"Well, you came to the right place. My cat had four kit-tens and two of them are yellow tabbies like Eva Jean's cat was."

He grinned. "I might just take both of them. They'd be company for each other while she's at work."

"Good idea."

"I knew if anybody in town had a kitten that needed a home, it'd be you. Maybe you ought to register yourself as a home for stray animals."

"Thanks, but there's enough here already." She slipped the halter off the horse's head and let him amble away. "I hope Bob is wrong about these horses. I'd like to see them healthy and in a good home. I've been handling them a lot to take away their fear of people."

"As warm weather gets here, they may perk up." Tom slapped the gun he wore strapped to his waist as if to check that it was still there. "Well, I've got to be running on, or I'll be late picking up Eva Jean. When can I get those kittens?"

"Anytime next week. They'll be weaned by then." She waved goodbye as he let himself out of the feed lot. She went in through the barn to put away the horse brush and halter, then headed for the house. Time had slipped away from her as it so often did. If she was going to reach Lucas's cabin by noon, she would have to hurry.

After washing her face and hands, she pulled her dark hair back in two barrettes and put on a clean blouse. As she prepared a picnic lunch of sandwiches and slices of pound cake she mentally went over the titles of books she had on hand. If Lucas wasn't much of a reader, she didn't want to embarrass him with Dostoyevski or Trollope. Nor did he look like the type to really get into Browning or Keats or Shelley. Thus she decided to compromise with some mysteries.

She packed the lunch in a camera bag, which she had learned made a perfect picnic basket when she was traveling by horse since the padded case prevented the sandwiches from being mashed. Then she saddled India, and slipped the books into the saddle bag. Looping the strap of the camera bag over the saddle horn, as she rode away calling out the afternoon's instructions to her two hired hands.

This time the back gate between her property and the land Lucas claimed he owned was easier to open, and as she rode toward the cabin, her heart was full of expectation.

Surely, she told herself, the man couldn't be as handsome as she had remembered, nor as tall and mysterious. She knew she had always had an overactive imagination and expected this would prove to be just one more instance in which what she remembered and how things were didn't match. But she hoped this wasn't the case. She had fallen asleep the night before, puzzling over why this good-looking man had chosen to be a hermit, then she'd dreamed about him.

She saw herself wearing a beautiful ball gown and dancing beneath an enormous crystal chandelier with a man who wore a military uniform. He moved her about the floor with great skill and when the dance was over, he led her out into a private garden. Then the man swept her into his arms and passionately kissed her. She knew he was the hermit, but when she asked his name, he faded into a mist and was gone.

She awoke from the dream at 5:00 a.m. with her heart pounding from the passion of his lips and an aching need to be back in his arms again. As she came to full consciousness she realized how foolish it was to have such strong feelings for a man she had just met. But then maybe this was another instance of being in the right place at the right time. It certainly wouldn't hurt to get to know him better and find out. Unable to go back to sleep, she had been up to see the sunrise, all the while reminding herself they were just neighbors.

As his cabin came in sight she slowed her pace and studied the scene. The cabin itself looked as if it had nestled in this place for a hundred years. The hand-hewn logs were silvered with age, and on the porch to the right of the front door was a wooden rocker that looked new, and to the left was a small stack of firewood. As there was no defined yard, the field grass, liberally infused with wildflowers, had grown all the way up to the wooden porch steps. Out back of the cabin was a lumpy plot that might have been a garden at one time, but obviously, the ground there hadn't been plowed in years as it was overgrown with grass.

As she dismounted and tied her horse to the porch rail, Lucas stepped out from the doorway. "You again!"

She smiled. "I told you I'd be back. Did you forget?" She was pleasantly surprised to find he was even more handsome than she had remembered, then realized that she was feeling somewhat apprehensive and didn't know why.

"I had hoped *you* would. Listen, I've got things—"

"Well, I didn't. I rarely forget anything. You know I can still remember the phone number our family had when I was a child." Nervously she changed subjects without taking a breath. "Would you like a dog?"

"I beg your pardon?"

"A dog. I noticed you don't have one, and I have some extras. Or maybe a couple of kittens? You can't have the two yellow ones because they're going to Eva Jean, but there's a black one and a spotted one." She knew she was talking too fast, but couldn't seem to stop. He was staring at her in a most unsettling way—not threatening, but intense.

"Are you always this confusing?"

"What do you mean?"

He came out onto the porch and leaned his forearms on the rail. "No, I don't want a dog or a cat."

"That's too bad. I have a red-bone coon hound that would be perfect with this cabin. I found him wandering on the highway, but he's perfectly healthy. You don't have to decide about the kittens until next week. They won't be ready until then." She wondered if his dark beard would feel soft or crisp. The recollection of his passionate kiss in her dream flooded her thoughts, and she had to avert her eyes before the memory caused her to blush.

Lucas studied her with cautious interest. She seemed sane enough, that is, until she opened her mouth to speak. And she was so pretty, he couldn't take his eyes from her. Not beautiful, at least not in the classic sense, but he suspected people who knew her were unaware of that. She seemed to be full of sunshine and butterflies.

"Well?" she asked.

"Well what?"

"Where do you want to go for our picnic?"

"I don't." He really didn't want to discourage her, but it had to be done.

"But I made sandwiches and pound cake. Look." She removed the camera bag from the saddle horn and held it up for him to see.

"You aren't planning to take my picture, are you?" he asked, moving back from the rail into the shadows.

"Of course not. Why would I do that? Oh, the camera bag. No. You see the food's in the camera bag. But look what I have over here." Rainie reached behind the saddle and brought out the contents of the saddlebag." See? I brought you some books." She thrust them toward him.

Gingerly Lucas stepped forward and took the books, then tilted them and examined the spines. "I've read these." Then he added, "Thanks anyway," and pushed them back toward her.

To his surprise she gazed up at him with pity. "I see."

"What? What do you see?"

"You really can't read and you don't want to admit it, so you say you've read the books already. Lucas, there's no reason for you to be embarrassed. A lot of adults never had anyone to teach them, especially here in the hills."

He stared at her. "Despite the conclusion you've jumped to, I can read."

"I understand," she replied in a sympathetic tone that clearly indicated her disbelief.

"Well, I can, damn it!" He pulled the books back from her and looked at them again. "In this one, the maiden aunt was the murderer, in this one it was the French spy, and in this one nobody did it, but in the confusion all the principle characters defect to America."

"Why, that's wonderful!"

"So you see, I can read, and there's no reason for you to be here." He kept his temper in check and decided to overlook the insult.

"Except for the picnic," she prompted. She looped the strap of the camera bag over her shoulder and was coming up the steps when he intercepted her. "Can't I come in?"

"Lady, you don't know me from Adam. Don't you know better than to go into a stranger's house?" He tried to leer at her in an alarming way, but she only smiled in return.

"Would you rather eat on the porch? That's fine with me. Or maybe down by the stream? Personally I prefer the stream."

Lucas ran his fingers through his hair as he often did when he was exasperated. "Okay. You win. We'll have lunch, then you'll go away, and we'll never see each other again. Agreed?"

She smiled, but made no promises.

The stream, only a few yards from the house, spread wide and clear but was shallow enough to wade in. Sunlight spangled its rapidly changing surface, and in an eddy next to the bank a school of minnows darted from sight at their approach. With no washtub in evidence, Rainie assumed the strange man must have to take his clothes into Roan Oak to be washed. "It must be difficult," she said.

"What must be?" He sat down on a flat sun-warmed rock and frowned at her.

"Living without electricity," she answered as she joined him.

He shrugged. "I've never been much of one to watch television. A kerosene lamp puts out enough light to allow me to read." He shot a look at her as if he expected her to challenge him again.

Rainie spread a large napkin on the rock between them and set out the sandwiches and pound cake. "Darn. I forgot to put in the chips."

"We don't need them." He took up a sandwich and peeled back the plastic wrap. "Looks good," he added grudgingly.

"Sandwiches aren't all that difficult." She peered into the bag. "Can you believe this? I went off and left the canned drinks on my counter, too."

"I have some."

"Great. Where are they, and I'll go get them."

"No," he stated rather abruptly, then stood and laid his sandwich on the rock. "You stay here and I'll go."

She watched as he crossed the clearing. He was every bit as tall as she had remembered, and a lot sexier. He moved with the grace of a natural athlete and had a presence about him as if he owned all he surveyed. She looked around and realized he actually did own it all, such as it was, if what he said was true. Absently she wondered if he had any income at all and if so, from what. He must have some, she reasoned, or he wouldn't have clean, neat clothes, and he would have cultivated that garden plot and been growing his own food. On the other hand, he would need very little to live here in his cabin without even electricity. This man was a far cry from wheeling-dealing Harry. And that made him all the more appealing.

Lucas returned with two canned drinks and a bag of potato chips. He handed her a can and popped the top of his own. "Sorry I can't offer you any ice. I don't have a refrigerator."

"No ice?" She looked at the can.

"I keep them in the root cellar, so it will be pretty cool. Just pretend you're in Europe."

Rainie opened the can and sipped it. "Not bad. How did you know you have to ask for ice in Europe?"

"I read a lot." He avoided her eyes and settled back onto the rock and picked up his sandwich.

"I'm sorry about that. I didn't mean to offend you." She leaned forward. "*Did* I offend you?"

He studied her, but made no reply.

"I must have." Rainie sighed. "I have the worst habit of doing that. Jumping to conclusions, I mean. And I do things on impulse. I have six scrawny horses to prove it!"

Lucas thoughtfully took a drink before he said, "Does that make sense? Did I miss something?"

"You saw one of them when we met. I found six horses that were being horribly mistreated, so I bought them all and had the owner arrested. Unfortunately they had to turn him loose again."

"Do you have other bridles than the one that horse is chewing in two?"

Rainie jerked her head around to find India's reins in his mouth. "India! You stop that!" To Lucas she said, "He doesn't like to be tied." In a louder voice, as if for the horse's benefit, she added, "But he can stop acting like a spoiled child and show some patience."

To Lucas's surprise the horse dropped the reins and tipped one of his back hooves as if he were preparing for a nap.

"I spoil all my animals," she confided. "I just can't seem to help it." She handed him another sandwich. "So have you lived here long?"

"My family has."

"I haven't. I grew up in San Antonio. Then I got married and moved to Louisville—Kentucky, that is."

"This is a pretty far ride from Louisville."

When she laughed, an intriguing dimple appeared in her chin. "I live here now. I've been here two years."

"And your husband?"

"I left him behind in Louisville. We're divorced. A friend of mine said she thinks he was remarried recently."

"No regrets?"

"Good heavens, no. I'm the one who divorced him, after all. I sort of feel sorry for whoever he married. There sure are a lot of floors to buff in that house. Harry is crazy about buffed floors."

He smiled and his features softened. "Then you aren't broken-hearted over the divorce and bitter because he found someone else?"

"I prefer carpets. Harry doesn't even like animals! Can you imagine that?" She paused and looked as if she might have said something else that would offend him. "Do you?"

"Like animals? Sure I do."

"I guess they can be pretty expensive to keep. On the other hand, cats are good at getting rid of mice and rats."

"I don't have mice and rats. Since I don't have cattle to feed, all my mice and rats moved down to your barn. So you see, it makes sense for you to keep the cats down there." Damn, he thought, I'm beginning to reason just like she does!

"I guess you're right."

She ate in silence for a few minutes, then said, "You know, it's funny, but when I first asked around town about buying this land, I was told a corporation owned it."

Lucas's eyes narrowed. "Oh?"

"But no one seemed to know who owns the corporation."

"Then I'd just assume everybody was mistaken. As you can see, I own this land."

"Obviously, but it's odd they would all be wrong. I mean, Lupine is like most small towns where everybody knows everybody else's business."

He shrugged. She was fascinating, and he wished he could get to know her better. But, of course, that was out of the question. He liked the way her blouse molded against her breasts. Yes, getting to know her better was definitely out of the question.

"I guess you were born right there in that cabin and maybe your parents and grandparents before you," she mused with one of her instant shifts of subject.

"My grandmother was born in the room there with the double window."

"In the back there? I thought that must be the bedroom."

He noticed the way the sunlight dancing in her hair accentuated its ruddy highlights. The shade from leaves overhead dappled her creamy complexion, and he wondered if her skin felt as soft as it looked. Hastily he averted his gaze.

"How old is this cabin?" she asked.

"The original room goes back to the early 1800s. A fire destroyed a shed on the back about the time the Civil War ended, and rather than just rebuild the back wall, they added another room. There's another addition on the far side that houses the bathroom."

"I wondered about that. I didn't see an outhouse."

"My grandmother insisted."

Rainie handed him a wedge of yellow pound cake. "Have you ever been off this mountain? To live, I mean? No," she answered herself. "I guess not. And I don't blame you. The Smokies are so much nicer than cities, at least they are in the ways I find important." She ate a bite of cake and added, "You haven't missed much."

Lucas let her believe whatever she pleased. After today he probably wouldn't see her again. She glanced sideways at him, and he couldn't help but notice she had the bluest eyes he had ever seen. A man could lose his soul in those eyes.

"Everybody ought to have a dream," she stated without preamble.

"I agree." He paused to see where her thoughts were leading this time.

"When I was a child, I wanted to be a veterinarian."

"That's an unlikely dream for a little girl. What changed your mind?"

"I got older and found out a vet doesn't get to keep all the animals he cures." She smiled at the memory. "So then I decided I wanted to have a horse ranch. Miles and miles of beautiful, rolling hills, and horses everywhere."

"Then your dream has come true?"

"On a small scale." She threw him off balance by asking, "What was your dream?"

"To be world-famous," he said without thinking.

She nodded sagely. "I guess all kids want that in one way or another. I was going to be a world-famous horse-raiser."

She laughed. "I didn't know there was no such thing. At least not one who is a common household name, like a movie star." She added, "Did you ever want to be a movie star?"

"Never. I can't act."

"You're so handsome I thought maybe you had."

He cut his eyes questioningly toward her, and his brow was furrowed.

She smiled to put him at ease, having no idea what she had said to startle him. "I guess that daydream is more prevalent with little girls than with little boys. My brothers wanted to be world-famous baseball players."

"And are they?"

"No, Andy sells insurance and Brian is an engineer. In an office, not on a train. Are you an only child?"

"I have one sister."

"It's a shame your parents are gone." When she saw his surprised look, she added, "I assumed they must be, since you live in the family house all alone."

"Yes. They're gone." This was true in one sense. They lived in Memphis, not in Lupine, and were on a Mediterranean cruise at the moment.

"Mine hoped I would come back to San Antonio, and I had expected to, but I saw Lupine on the way there and decided this was where I wanted to be."

He looked confused. "You left Louisville, Kentucky, on your way to San Antonio, Texas, and passed through Lupine, Tennessee?"

"I've never been very good at maps. And anyway, I was in no hurry. Life with Harry hadn't exactly been one long adventure. I would have found Texas eventually."

Lucas grinned and shook his head from side to side. "You're certainly the most unusual woman I've ever met."

"Am I? Harry said I reminded him more of Nutsy the Flying Squirrel than anyone he knew. I don't think he meant it as a compliment."

"I did. I like your uniqueness." He was also aware of a genuineness she possessed, especially by comparison to all the other women he had known.

"You do?" Her lips parted in a smile, and he could see the even row of her white teeth. "I like you, too."

His smile vanished. "You can't like me. What I mean is, we aren't going to be friends. You insisted we have lunch together, and that's all there is to it." He tried to look stern and foreboding.

"Well, that's just silly. We like each other and we're neighbors so we may as well be friends."

"No way. I'm not in the market for any friends."

She tilted her head to one side. "You know, you sure don't talk like a hermit."

"What's that supposed to mean?"

"I would assume that a man who lived all by herself on top of a mountain without TV or radio or anything wouldn't speak so correctly."

He blinked as he wondered how to reply to that.

"I guess it's the reading. A person can educate himself pretty well by reading. Is that it?"

"I don't want—"

"But where do you get books? Is there a library in Roan Oak? There isn't in Lupine."

"The county seat has a library." If she wanted to believe he was self-educated, let her.

"You drive all the way over there? I'm surprised your Jeep will take you that far."

He followed her gaze to the derelict Jeep under the shed. "Appearances can be deceiving."

"Now see? That doesn't sound like something a hermit would say."

"I doubt you've known enough hermits to make a qualified comparison."

"That's true," she admitted. "You're my first."

Lucas found himself gazing deep into her bewitching blue eyes. They were the shade that he usually associated with velvet and were rimmed with the longest black eyelashes he had ever seen. Her lips were the color of dewy roses and seemed to draw him like a lodestone. Against all logic he found himself leaning toward her.

For the eternity of a heartbeat they each held their breath as something new and exciting blossomed between them. Lucas forced himself to inhale and drew back, breaking the fragile moment.

He felt unsettled, and from the way she was gazing off into the distance, she felt it, too. He had almost kissed her. He wished that he had.

Abruptly he stood and turned his back to distance himself, but the memory of her haunting blue eyes and parted lips stayed with him.

"I'm sorry I called you a hermit."

"What?" He turned and looked down at her.

Rainie looked confused and embarrassed as she gathered up the remains of their lunch. He noticed her hands were trembling. "I guess that's not a flattering term," she said.

"I'm not upset about that. Forget it." His voice sounded harsh in his effort to control himself. He still wanted to put his arms around her.

"Then why are you upset?"

He frowned at her. "I'm not upset."

"Yes, you are."

He drew a deep breath. "You're right. I am. I'm upset because you're invading my privacy."

"No, that's not it."

He glared at her. "What do you mean that's not it? I ought to know why I'm upset, shouldn't I?"

"Yes, I would think so, but if that was it, you wouldn't have agreed to share a picnic with me or have thought about kissing me."

"I never did!"

"I'm not blind, Lucas. I can tell when a man wants to kiss me and when he doesn't." She stood in front of him, her fists balled on her slender hips.

"You're a crazy lady. You know that? Now go away and leave me alone."

To his surprise tears gathered like crystals in her eyes. "Do you really mean that?"

Lucas felt his heart melt, and he took a step toward her. She tilted her head up to meet his eyes. She was so small and looked so vulnerable, he ached to hold her. He had never meant to make her cry. "Look. All I want is my privacy. It's very important to me. Until you wandered in here, no one knew I was here, and that's the way I like it."

"No one?"

"Now all I'm asking is that you honor my privacy and go away. I like you, but I don't want to be your friend. Okay?"

"And you think *I'm* confusing?" She blinked away her tears. "If you like me, why don't you want to get to know me better? I like you, and I'd like to know more about you."

"People are different," he said, grasping at straws. "When I like somebody, that's it. I don't want to keep seeing them or I might find out I don't like them, after all."

"That's weird!"

He threw up his hands. "I guess that's what makes me a hermit. Who can figure it?"

"So does that mean you only see those people you don't like?"

"Nope. Why hang out with somebody like that? No, I just stay up here by myself and contemplate all the people—like you—that I like but avoid."

"And you like it this way?"

"You'd better believe it."

"I wish you had."

"What? Had what?"

"Kissed me." She smiled. "You might have had something really pleasant to contemplate then." Before he could stop her, she turned and walked toward her horse.

Lucas stared after her. "Hey, wait a minute."

She paused and looked back.

"You're going? Just like that?"

"Isn't that what you wanted?"

He drew himself up. "Of course it is."

"Okay." She turned back and went to her horse. She slipped the strap of her camera bag over the saddle horn and untied the reins. Lucas watched her rounded derriere as she raised her leg high to put her foot in the stirrup, then swung into the saddle. The way Rainie moved made the simple acts of mounting her horse seductive. Incredibly, she seemed to be taking his far-out explanation at face value.

"Wait a minute," he heard himself saying. "I guess it's okay if you come back once in a while." He pointed his finger at her warningly. "But not too often! I'm still a hermit."

She smiled and nudged her horse into a lope.

Lucas watched as the woods swallowed her up. She hadn't said if she would return or not, and for some reason this made him want to run after her.

With a growl, he wheeled and stalked back to his cabin. Nutsy the Flying Squirrel was an apt description!

Despite his better judgment, he hoped he would see her again.

3

"MARLA, I MET the most fascinating man!"

With a smile, Marla looked up from the list of wedding guests. "Oh! Here in Lupine?"

"Sort of. He lives between here and Roan Oak. His name is Lucas Dalton."

"Like the outlaws? I don't know any Daltons."

"He shops in Roan Oak. It's probably more accessible to his place than Lupine." Rainie slid lower on the couch so that her head rested on its cushioned back; her stockinged feet were nestled beneath her. "He's even more handsome than what's-his-name in that movie we just saw."

"Who isn't? I'll be glad when anti-heroes go out of style and leading men become romantic and handsome again. I was going through withdrawal until I became addicted to old movies."

"Bob is handsome," Rainie stated loyally.

"Bob is marvelous, but he isn't handsome. He looks like a redheaded, freckled-faced boy all grown up." She touched her own strawberry-blond hair. "All our kids will probably look like the Freckled Farkels."

Raine laughed. "I remember them. You and Bob will have adorable children."

With a smile, Marla went back to checking names off her list. "Tell me about this Dalton person."

"I don't know much about him. He's a bit of a recluse and says he's lived on the mountain all his life. Apparently he and all his family were born right there in his log cabin."

"He lives in a log cabin?"

Rainie nodded. "A real one. Not a modern log home, but a genuine log cabin. The logs have ax marks on them."

"Didn't we send an invitation to Eva Jean? She's not on this list."

"I addressed it myself." Rainie sighed in pleasant recollection. "Lucas is so . . . mysterious. I've never met anyone like him."

"There are some pretty strange characters living back in the hills. How do you suppose Eva Jean's name was left off this list? I hope I haven't forgotten anyone . . ." She wrinkled her nose as she studied the list.

"I had a picnic with him yesterday."

"Who? The mountain man?"

"Lucas. We ate by a stream near his cabin. I'll be going back to see him again soon."

"Are you sure that's a good idea? If he's such a recluse, maybe you shouldn't trust him."

"That's silly, Marla. He can't help it if he lives in a remote place—it's family land. Besides, he's so shy he can barely carry on a conversation. I do most of the talking."

"So what's new?" her friend quipped with a grin.

"I'm not that bad. Where's Bob tonight? With the wedding only a couple of weeks away, I thought for sure he would be over here."

"One of Tom Hanford's prize cows is having a difficult labor. He may come by later."

"Do you think Tom and Eva Jean will ever get married?" Rainie asked as she toyed with the fringe on a throw pillow.

"Not unless she arranges everything and sends him a special invitation. They've dated for so long, I think they're in a rut."

"Someone told me they were high-school sweethearts, and Tom is what? In his late thirties?"

"That's right. They both are."

Rainie nodded. "That's a long time of waiting to see if it will last."

"What about you? Have you ever thought of remarrying?"

"Bob asked me the same thing. I told him if I did, it wouldn't be to another Harry." Thoughts of how dissimilar Lucas was from Harry popped into her mind. "But I'd also have to find a man who'd be willing to put up with my eccentricities."

"Eccentricities? You seem pretty normal to me."

"How many husbands would put up with a wife buying six starving horses on the spur of the moment just because she felt sorry for them? What about the time I had to set my alarm every two hours to bottle-feed those abandoned kittens? And the raccoon I took in until his broken leg healed? And the goat I had with epileptic seizures?"

"Maybe *you* should be the one marrying Bob."

"I have many and varied needs for the services of a veterinarian, but not for a husband. Besides, he wouldn't marry me. He'd be losing one of his best clients."

"All the same, I'm sure there are men who would find your compassion for animals an endearing trait and wouldn't mind at all. What about your recluse? He's bound to love animals, since he's isolated himself from people."

"He doesn't even own a cat or a dog. Can you imagine? I'd go bananas up there without any animals or people at all."

"That does seem unusual. Most farmers keep at least a watchdog and a cat or two to keep down the mice."

"He's not a farmer. There's a place out back that looks as if it used to be a garden, but he hasn't plowed it."

"How odd." Marla rested her chin on her hand. "Even I have a sunny spot for tomatoes and bell peppers. Once I move to Bob's place, I plan to have a full garden."

"Not everybody is into gardening, I suppose," Rainie admitted, "but it did seem odd to me at the time. I guess he buys all he needs."

"I suppose he must." Marla reached for a magazine and showed Rainie a picture of a bridesmaid's dress. "Are you sure Betty Franks will look good in this shade of blue? You can wear it, but her hair is that dark blond color, you know."

Rainie nodded. "She'll look pretty in it. This shade would be flattering on anyone. Besides, it's too late now. Mrs. Franks will have them ready for the final fittings on Monday."

"I know. I guess I've just got the last-minute jitters. Not only is my mother driving me crazy by inviting everyone she has ever spoken to in her life, but this is my last weekend as a single woman. A week from Saturday I'll be Mrs. Bob Pollard. Marla Pollard. Do you think that sounds okay?"

Rainie pretended to be trying to decide. "No, I think you should dye these dresses bright red and marry someone else."

Marla laughed and threw the nearest pillow at her friend. "You're a big help!"

Rainie glanced at the wall clock. "It's getting late. I ought to be going."

"Is it midnight already?" Marla asked in surprise as she followed Rainie's gaze. "I had no idea."

As Rainie put on her jacket Marla added, "Does it bother you, going into a dark house so far out of town?"

"Of course not. I leave a light on, and I have dogs all over the place." She picked up her purse. "Before long you'll live in the country, too. Does that worry you?"

"No, not really. I guess I'll get used to it. After all, living in a town the size of Lupine is almost the same as being in the country."

Rainie bid her friend good-night and went out to her car. Marla might think it was the same, but Rainie knew it wasn't. Lupine was small, but there were neighboring houses here and streetlights. She knew Marla was nervous about the move and decided she would visit her often when Bob was out on a call. She could use company herself.

Lupine's lights were soon left behind, and the thick black of the nighttime countryside enveloped her. Rainie wasn't afraid of living alone, at least not usually, but she couldn't say it didn't bother her at times. The loneliness frequently got to her.

In only a few minutes she rolled to a stop out front of her home. The farmhouse she lived in was vintage 1930s, with wide porches, tall windows and a steeply pitched tin roof. After the first few rainstorms, she was convinced she should replace the tin with some other, quieter roofing material, but hadn't yet gotten around to it.

As usual there were four or five dogs of various sizes and breeds sleeping on the front porch, and typically, none of them bothered to bark at a car driving up. As Rainie threaded her way over and around the dogs, one of them raised his head and beat a welcome to her with his tail. Another sighed deeply in his undisturbed sleep. "It's a good thing I'm not a burglar," she scolded as she unlocked the door. "You dogs are a disgrace."

The table lamp she'd left on lit her way across a large, comfortable living room. The house had been designed for a family with several children, and thus all the rooms were spacious. She had furnished the house with country antiques and overstuffed chairs and a sofa. Most of the wooden furniture was either pine or oak, and all the pieces had been used and enjoyed by people for years. On one wall hung a beautifully crafted quilt, on another was a collection of old samplers, most of them browned and stained with age.

For Rainie, the house usually felt warm and friendly, a great contrast to the chrome-and-glass museum she had shared with Harry. However the house seemed too empty tonight, and she wasn't sure why. Perhaps, she thought, it was all the talk with Marla about wedding plans. She was happy for her friends, but although she would never admit it to them, she was inwardly envious.

As she went down the hall to her bedroom her steps seemed overly loud on the hardwood floors. She flipped on the bedroom light and turned on the small TV across from her bed, but the inane dialogue from the rerun of a twenty-year-old detective show only seemed to emphasize her loneliness. She didn't miss Harry—she was never *that* lonely—but she was missing...someone. Someone who would look up and smile when she came into the room. Someone who would hold her in his arms during all the lonely nights. Maybe that someone was Lucas Dalton, she thought. But he had said he didn't want to be her friend, even though he admitted he liked her.

With a frown she stared at her big, brass bed with its neatly stitched quilt and downy comforter. If she hadn't fallen in love with the bed's old-fashioned charm, she would never have bought such a large one.

Somewhat listlessly, Rainie crossed to her pine wardrobe, took out a cotton gown, and began getting ready for bed. She was young, and she had all the normal desires of a woman; she wasn't willing to accept the idea of a future all alone. But if things didn't work out with Lucas—and she had no valid reason to expect they would, given his attitude—and if she stayed in Lupine, what else could she expect?

There weren't any others here she would even remotely consider marrying. Yet she loved the sleepy little community and its protecting mountains. In the two years she'd been here, she had formed friendships closer and more precious to her than any she had made in the eight years she'd lived in Louisville. In Lupine everyone knew everyone else, and they were all considered important. No, she didn't want to move away.

Naked, she went to the bathroom, tossed her clothes in the laundry hamper, and brushed the tangles from her hair before coming back into the bedroom and slipping on her cambric gown. The fabric was soft against her skin and was romantically styled with lace at the throat and at the gathered cuffs. It was a shame, she thought, that no man had ever seen it—or was likely to.

With a sigh she turned off the light and television set and went to bed. In the darkness that enfolded her, she could hear the barely audible sounds of the old house settling for the night. An owl hooted in the distance, and the wind rustled in the lilac bush outside her window. Familiar sounds, all of them, but not one was the sound of a lover. *That* was what she wanted, she realized. A lover. And preferably one who was also her husband.

She rolled to her side and drew up her knees. Lucas Dalton was unquestionably all she could ask for in terms of physical appearance, and she did seem to have a love of nature in common with him, although she wasn't sure about whether he cared as much for animals as she did. But he had also insisted that she leave him alone and not invade his privacy. Had he meant that, or was he just shy and uncomfortable socially? She would never know unless she spent more time with him. And, after all, what did she have to lose?

LUCAS GLARED at the blank page in the typewriter, fuming in frustration, then he shoved himself away from the table and paced the cabin's width several times before dropping back onto the chair. He strained to think of a word, *any* word, that would start his brain flowing, but again, nothing came. With a growl he rose again and resumed pacing.

This had become his usual working routine, or rather, his non-working routine. He hadn't been able to string together an entire paragraph in almost a month.

Writer's block. The nemesis that all writers feared. The thought paralysis that could come on without warning and stay. Anything from personal problems to world crises could bring it on, and no one seemed sure what made it go away. Lucas's had come about because of a deadline.

He had had many deadlines in his career, some of his own making, some dictated by his publishing house, but before now, none of them had ever fazed him.

He had weathered a bad marriage and had survived a divorce that surely would rival Armageddon, yet he had been able to continue his highly creative work through it all. His friends had marveled at his ability to focus his thoughts on his work at such a stressful time. He tried to explain to them that the fiction he wrote was an escape, that it took him to a world where Christine and all the problems related to her didn't exist, but he was never sure they understood.

After a year's struggle, the divorce had been settled and property divisions made and lawyers paid. Not long after that, his agent had made a deal with a prestigious publishing house for the rights to his next novel, with an advance against royalties well into six figures, and a movie option to boot. And that was when Lucas developed writer's block.

"This is crazy!" he yelled up at the rafters. "Why *now*?"

He pulled the paper out of the typewriter, turned it over and rolled it back in. It looked the same on that side as it had on the other. No ideas sprang forth.

He picked up the dog-eared copy of the synopsis of the novel he'd written several months before and re-read it, though he had long since memorized it word for word. The plot sounded trite, the characters sappy. What the hell had his agent and editor seen in this? Why had he ever thought it was a good idea in the first place? He threw the papers back down.

Restlessly he paced to the cabin's front window, and as he stared across the clearing he tried again to convince himself that he was glad the crazy lady on the black horse hadn't shown up again. She was a distraction he was sure he didn't need. But then, everything distracted him lately—the words on cereal boxes, the patent number on his stapler, the number of rubber bands in the box, the dust that collected beneath the keys on his typewriter. He had spent one entire day taking the machine apart and cleaning it, and for all his effort, he still received no inspiration.

When he had incorporated as Wyndfell, Inc., naming his company after the title of his first novel, he had never pictured such an ignoble conclusion. Lucas Dalton, a.k.a. Jordan Lane, dead of writer's block at the pinnacle of his career. It was enough to make him swear, but he'd already tried that to no avail.

The cabin should have been the answer. He had always felt inspired here. Despite his upbringing in Memphis and the years he had lived in cities, his soul belonged to the Smoky Mountains. His heart was here, but where was his creativity?

The idea for the trip to the mountain cabin had occurred to him one sleepless night, almost as if it were an inspiration. Without another thought, he wrote a note for his housekeeper, and before dawn he was on his way to Lupine. His cabin had no TV or stereo to distract him, and he took no books other than the ones he needed for research. There wasn't even a telephone to seduce him into calling friends or letting them call him. There was nothing at all to do but write. But after a whole month, he didn't have so much as one page to show for it.

The deadline was looming in his future. In his imagination it had taken on a life and character of its own. Lucas was as purely professional as any writer he knew, and he consid-

ered all deadlines as sacrosanct. If he said he would deliver a
manuscript by a certain date, he did it even if it meant working around the clock and on weekends. But this deadline was
more formidable than most—it had writer's block in its corner.

For a fleeting moment Lucas considered abandoning this
idea and starting on a fresh one, but the thought of the huge
advance involved and the movie option, as well as having to
explain to his agent, dissuaded him.

With a groan, he went back to the typewriter and sat down.
Burying his face in his hands he tried to recall the methods
his writer friends had said they'd used to overcome this crip-
pling problem. He had tried them all, and none had worked
for him.

"Who the hell do I think I'm kidding?" he demanded of the
blank page. "I can't write, and I never could. All my other
books were just flukes!" That made him feel more justified,
but since he had written two dozen books, all of which had
made the *New York Times* best-seller list, his logical mind
questioned the statement's validity.

He got up again and went to the butane stove and made
another pot of coffee. Since coming to this mountaintop he
had singularly consumed enough coffee to put Juan Valdez
on easy street. Once more he glanced out into his yard. No
one.

Although he hated admitting it, he missed her. How he
could miss someone he had only seen twice, he wasn't sure,
but he did. Maybe, he thought, it was because she was a di-
version. One of those things he had come here to avoid. But
he knew better. Rainie Sheenan would have intrigued him no
matter where he might have met her.

Intrigue was putting it mildly. Haunting, obsessing, com-
pelling—these were more accurate descriptions. She had been
on his mind day and night in the three days since he had seen

her. Why hadn't she come back? Surely she wasn't a figment of his imagination—not when his imagination was so blocked he couldn't create a story when he had the outline right in front of him. No, she was real.

For a minute he considered walking down to her place to simply say hello. Only that. No complications. Then he could leave and come back to wrestle with his writer's block again. The exercise would be good for him.

No! He pulled himself up short. That was his demon talking again. It would do anything to keep him from writing! He was developing a wary respect for such a formidable enemy.

As he sipped his coffee he seesawed between reinforcing his writer's block and wondering what it would have been like to kiss her.

A movement caught his eye, and he leaned toward the window. As if his thoughts had manifested her, there she was, riding into his clearing! He got up so fast, coffee sloshed onto the tabletop. Hastily he grabbed a paper napkin and wiped up the spill, then hurried across the room, hoping to reach the door before she did.

"You must have radar," she commented as he stepped out to greet her. "I never get as far as your porch."

"You came back."

"Very good, Lucas. You're right." She gave him a pixieish smile. "Did you miss me?"

"No," he lied.

She looked at him quizzically. "Don't you get bored up here? What do you do all day?"

"I try to think up ways to discourage trespassers and do away with the more persistent ones." Although his lips weren't smiling, his eyes were.

"That sounds interesting. What would you like to do with me?"

He looked away. "If you raise horses, why do you always ride this same one?"

"The others come and go. India is my personal favorite."

"India?"

"I named him that because he's as black as India ink, all but the white stripe on his face."

"He's beautiful."

"Don't say it in front of him. He's conceited enough as it is." So Lucas did have an appreciation for horses, she thought as she stroked the warm velvet of the animal's neck. "Well? Are you going to ask me in?"

"No!" Lucas snapped as he thought of the typewriter and the other paraphernalia he had scattered about. Experience had proved to him that women saw him in a different light when they learned he was also Jordan Lane.

She looked at him curiously.

"The house is a mess," he offered as an excuse. "I'm not used to having company."

"Is that all? I don't mind."

"I do. Let's sit out here." He pulled the rocker around for her so she would be facing away from the window. "You sit here." He lowered himself onto the top porch step.

After an awkward pause he said, "How have you been keeping busy? I guess you have a boyfriend."

"Actually I don't. Don't you think it's a shame we have to go on using 'boyfriend' and 'girlfriend' when we're adults? Looks as if somebody would invent a new word. Aren't there people who do that?"

"I suppose writers do," he answered carefully.

"Maybe so. Now that so many adults are dating, I hope someone comes up with one soon. No, I don't have one."

"Word?"

"Boyfriend. I have several men friends, but nobody that I see romantically. I assume that's what you meant?"

"It was just a casual question. I don't care one way or the other."

"Neither do I. That's why I don't have one. Do you have a girlfriend? No, of course not, or you couldn't be a hermit."

"There are rules?" he asked with a smile.

"There must be. Otherwise just anybody could be one simply by saying 'I'm a hermit.' After a while it wouldn't mean a thing." She leaned her head back on the rocker and set the chair in motion with her toe. "I've been busy with my horses. We're breaking one of the colts, and he's proving to be a handful."

"We?"

"I have two men working for me."

"I see."

"Do you ride?"

"I used to."

She smiled. "Would you like to ride with me some day?"

"No." He couldn't continue to let her distract him from his typewriter, but it hadn't made much difference lately as even his days alone were totally unproductive.

"Great. I'll bring an extra horse with me before too long. I can tell you like horses or you wouldn't feel so comfortable with India nibbling at your tennis shoe."

Lucas reached out and stroked the horse's soft nose. "Yeah, I like horses. Sometimes I wish I had one, but..." He stopped. He couldn't tell her who he was and that he didn't really live here all the time.

"Seems as if you would. With all these meadows you'd only have to feed it in the winter."

He tried to look distressed. "Horse feed costs money. Then there are vet bills and blacksmiths..."

"You wouldn't need shoes on one if you only ride on dirt and don't ride him hard every day." She looked at him in a calculating way. "Maybe we could work out a trade. I'll give you a horse and take care of its shots and shoes, if you'll let me use your meadow." If he would agree, they would be seeing a lot more of each other.

"I don't want a horse. Besides, you raise show horses and that would be too expensive a gift."

Undaunted, she countered, "Pasture land is expensive, too." She thought for a minute. "I happen to have a bay—he's one of my refugees. He'll be a beauty if he lives. Maybe you'd be comfortable with taking that one."

"If he lives?"

"Bob isn't too sure, but Bob tends to be pessimistic sometimes. The bay is the best of the six in my opinion."

"I have no idea what you're talking about."

"Come down to my place sometime, and I'll show you. Maybe you'll like the coon hound and the kittens, as well."

"I don't want any animals. I like knowing I can just pick up and leave any time I please."

"I understand." Her voice was filled with compassion, as if she assumed he would never travel farther than the county seat.

Perversely Lucas found himself wanting to tell her about himself, his real life, so she'd know he wasn't to be pitied. In most circles he was considered a celebrity. In anyone's opinion he was a wealthy man.

Why did he want to impress her, he mentally argued, when that would only lead to more involvement and more distraction? And, besides, she seemed quite taken with the impoverished Lucas Dalton, and he was sure it was more than just pity.

Rainie gazed at him, wondering why he seemed so mysterious. He didn't sound or act like a man who would choose to live without any social contact. She was even beginning to doubt his alleged trips to the county seat, because from where she sat on the porch, the rusty Jeep appeared incapable of taking him anywhere. Why would he lie about that unless it was to impress her? And he wouldn't be trying to impress her if he didn't care what she thought of him.

This strange man fascinated her. He was like one of the pioneers who had tamed the wilderness. Even his name, Lucas Dalton, sounded tough and a bit dangerous. He was powerfully built, too. Not beefy like a football player, but well-proportioned, as if he lifted weights in a supervised gym. That, of course, was ridiculous. There wasn't anything like that in Lupine or Roan Oak.

Her eyes settled on his lips. She fancied she could tell a lot about a person by his eyes, lips and hands. Lucas's mouth looked as if he smiled often, which begged the question of why he would smile up here all by himself, unless he was a happy person by nature. And his lips looked sensuous, as if he would be a master at lovemaking.

She lowered her gaze to his hands. Even in repose they appeared to be strong, as if he used them often. But they weren't rough and square like a farmer's hands. The fingers were long and looked artistic, but in a masculine way. His veins and tendons were clearly visible beneath the tanned skin across the back of his hands. His fingernails were cut short and were clean. If there was one thing Rainie objected to in a man, it was long nails. Even her own were no longer than the ends of her fingers.

His eyes were the telling part. Eyes revealed their secrets, if one knew how to look for them. Lucas's eyes were dark brown with a reddish hue and were as clear and as full of life as a child's. She sensed a deep intelligence there, as well, as if he had a thirst to know more than he had time to learn, and as if he forgot little of whatever he assimilated. His eyes didn't seem to go with his life as a recluse.

"Why are you staring at me?"

Rainie sat up and stammered, "I'm not. I mean, I didn't mean to stare. After all, you're sitting right there in front of me and I have to look somewhere, don't I?" Feeling guilty she added, "Sorry."

"That's okay. I just don't like people staring at me." For a minute there he'd thought she had recognized him. His face was on the dust jackets of two dozen books. For the sake of his anonymity, he was glad she hadn't, but his ego was suffering. He smiled as he realized he was being foolish to want it both ways.

Her skin looked so smooth, he wondered how it would feel to touch her. To kiss her. He yanked his thoughts into line.

The wind had picked up as evening approached and the temperature was dropping fast. Springtime in the mountains could be decidedly cool. He noticed Rainie had wrapped her arms across herself for warmth. He wished he could ask her in to sit by the fire, but evidence of Jordan Lane was all over the place. "Are you cold?"

"It's . . . invigorating."

"Bracing," he responded. "Cool wind is good for you. Builds character."

"Why do people say that?" she asked. "What real virtue is there in cold showers and sleeping with a window open so you freeze all night?"

"I guess to prove to yourself that you can take it."

"I must be a sissy. I like warm showers and a bedroom where I don't have to wear flannel granny gowns and pile tons of quilts on top of me."

Lucas felt his mouth go dry. His active imagination conjured up a picture of her in the shower with soft clouds of steam rising around her slick, naked body. And he could see her in a wide bed, her eyes dreamy from lovemaking—his lovemaking—and her not needing any gown or cover at all.

He swallowed and shifted his weight on the porch step. He couldn't want her! If he did, he couldn't have her!

Rainie leaned her head back, affording him a profile of her forehead, straight nose, rounded lips and chin, and the sweeping curve of her throat. In the open neck of her blouse he also saw the gentle mound of her breasts. "I love this time of day," she was saying. "It's as if nature is winding down and settling in for the night. Do you feel it?"

He nodded, then realized her eyes were closed. "Yes, I feel it. It's like one mood flowing into another. As if the world is making peace with itself before darkness comes."

She opened her eyes and looked at him. "That's very poetic."

"Maybe I read it somewhere." He had used that description in *Homeward*.

"Seems as if I have, too."

He held his breath until she shook her head. "I don't remember. Anyway, it's a lovely thing to say."

"Maybe you could come up for dinner some night," he said before he could stop himself.

"I'd love to. When?"

"Or maybe that's a bad idea. I mean, a bachelor living all alone, Lord knows what I might cook. Right?" He tried to smile.

"It will be an adventure. You know, it's funny that you said 'dinner' and not 'supper.' Around here people eat dinner at noon."

"And if you're here that late, it would mean you having to find your way back home through the woods in the dark. How foolish of me. Forget it."

"No problem. I'll bring a flashlight. India can find the barn and his feed trough blindfolded."

"I'm not much of a cook at all. I mainly live on Spam sandwiches."

"If you eat it, so can I." She gave him a warm smile. "You needn't be shy with me."

"Shy?" Lucas had been called a lot of things, but shy was not one of them.

"What evening should I come?"

"Well, I don't—"

"Of course I guess one is pretty much like another to you, isn't it? I have plans tomorrow night. I'm going to a wedding shower for my friend, Marla Cane."

"Darn! Wouldn't you know it? Tomorrow is the only night I'm—"

"So I'll come the next night. Okay?"

He looked at her through the gathering dusk and his heart beat double time. In this light her skin was pure gold and her eyes were the shade of violets. "Okay," he said.

Rainie got up and untied her horse. Using the porch as a mounting block, she dropped into the saddle. "I'm looking forward to seeing you again."

Lucas found he was grinning as she rode away. He had certainly never met anyone like her before.

Resolutely he turned back to the cabin and went in to resume his battle with the deadline monster.

4

RAINIE SETTLED COMFORTABLY into the saddle, but kept her eyes on the sorrel's pitched ears. This was the first time the horse had been ridden, and it paid to be careful. As with all Rainie's stock, the animal had been gently handled and loved since birth, but this one had the distinction of having been the first colt born on the Rainbow Ranch. Now he was two years old and ready to train for the saddle.

"You ought to let Billy get on him first," the older man repeated. "It don't hurt a teenage boy to get throwed." He gave a comradely wink at his seventeen-year-old co-worker.

"Blaze won't throw me," she said.

"No? Then you better get him to moving around instead of standing there thinking of meanness."

When Rainie nudged the horse's sides with her heels, his ears shot back, his aristocratic nostrils flared, and he arched his neck proudly. Then with a stiff-legged gait, he stalked across the arena.

"Better keep him moving," Billy called out. "Keep his head up."

"Billy, I've ridden all my life and—" Just at that instant, Blaze bowed his back, kicked his heels and launched himself a good three yards ahead, separating himself from his rider. Rainie landed in an undignified heap where the horse had been.

Gingerly she moved her legs, checking to be sure no bones were broken, and even before she had gotten to her knees, her two hired hands were by her side to help her to her feet. Her rear end hurt, but the greatest injury had been to her pride.

"I reckon I'd better ride him now," Billy said, managing to keep a straight face.

"That's not necessary," Rainie replied with determination as she crossed the pen and retrieved the horse. She ached all over, but she wasn't about to let this horse, or any horse, get the best of her.

This time, as soon as she was in the saddle, she kicked the horse into a rough lope. Blaze again tried to buck, but she wouldn't allow him to stay in one spot long enough for his efforts to be effective, nor would she let him slow down. After several minutes, she felt his muscles relax beneath her, and when his ears flicked forward, she knew the worst was over. Cautiously she allowed him to settle back in the running trot for which his breed was famous.

A broad grin covered her face. Riding this horse was as smooth as rocking in a chair. Her instincts had been right about not gelding this particular colt. Blaze's confirmation had proved to be excellent, and now that she knew he had also inherited his dame's championship quality gaits, she would keep him for breeding and for show.

Remaining watchful of him, she decided to let him pick his gaits as long as he kept moving and stayed relaxed. In time he would be taught to sustain each of them at the option of his rider, but for her first time in his saddle, it was enough to know he could find the gaits naturally.

When his neck began to darken with sweat, Rainie taught him to rein to a stop. For the next few minutes she practiced reining him from side to side and halting him, then she dismounted and removed his saddle and blanket. After taking off his bridle, she slipped his halter over his head and fastened his lead rope to the circling arm of the walker, which would keep him moving slowly so his muscles would gradually cool down.

"He's going to be a great asset," she said to Billy and Oscar. "By the time he reaches his prime we'll be able to get an impressive stud fee for him. We're becoming completely self-supporting."

"He looks good now, but he's just starting out," Oscar sagely cautioned as he stroked the stubble of beard on his chin. "If I were you, I wouldn't put so much stock in him until he's proved himself in a show or two."

Rainie chose to ignore the conservative observation of her hired hand. Granted he was older than she was and had worked with horses more years than she had, but her instincts had served her well in the past, and she had no reason to doubt them now.

"Are you still thinking about adding a herd of quarter horses?" Billy asked as he carried her tack back into the barn. "Maybe we ought to stick to what we know."

"I'll hire somebody else to work with them. You and Oscar are great with saddle horses, and I won't ask you to give them up. My main problem is in getting enough land. I'm hemmed in here."

"Maybe you could find out the name of whoever runs the company that owns that land up the mountain," Oscar suggested. "That spread would be perfect."

"When I first moved here, I was told it was owned by a corporation, but I'm not so sure that's right," she said as she thought of Lucas's claim to ownership.

"I heard somebody say the company's name once. It was real odd. Wind Field or something like that."

"Yes, that's what I remember. At the time I thought it sounded vaguely familiar, but I don't know where I would ever have heard of it before."

Oscar shrugged. "Maybe they make saddle soap or feed or something."

"Wind Field," she murmured again. Maybe, she thought, Lucas was only an overseer for someone else's property and had been too proud to admit it. She decided to go to the county library to check it out.

By midafternoon the soreness from Rainie's fall had penetrated deep into her muscles, but she was determined not to let the men know. They had a respect for her that encouraged her not to give in to bumps and bruises. She had seen both men bruised all over from being kicked or thrown or mashed against stalls, and they never complained. Aches and pains were a by-product of horse training.

Leaving them to exercise the horses that she and Billy would ride in the next show, she drove to the county seat. The library was housed within the imposing granite courthouse—the only building in town that looked as if it had been designed by an architect. All the rest of the businesses were housed in square, flat-faced buildings, with only the occasional pediment to break the horizontal roof lines. Nothing here but the courthouse inspired even a second look.

The courthouse, perched atop a man-made hill, had broad marble steps rising up each of its four identical sides. Years of wear had eroded the front edge of each step to the point where the center of the step appeared to be sagging, and the copper railings alongside had long ago taken on a soft green patina. Inside, the building was cool and dark and smelled faintly of yellowing papers and stale cigarette smoke. The interior stairways were hollowed even more deeply, and where the rails were often touched by passing hands, the copper gleamed. The first time Rainie had gone there, she'd been curious about the greater wear on the inside steps, but after seeing the heavy flow of traffic from floor to floor inside the building, she'd understood.

Because the library was on the floor below street level, it was cavelike and eerily silent, especially so because even whispers were discouraged. She much preferred a more modern library such as the one in Louisville, but any library was better than none at all.

Rainie had been here often, and as she entered she waved a silent greeting to the young woman behind the counter. The woman smiled in return.

Rainie prided herself on being able to find her way through any library, but even with the librarian's help, she was unable to locate any reference at all to a corporation with the name of Wind Field. There wasn't even a name that was similar.

"I guess I was given the wrong name," she finally admitted.

"That must be it. As I said, it might help if you knew what sort of product this company manufactures or what sort of service they provide."

Rainie smiled as if it wasn't all that important. "I'll ask around and see if anyone knows of it by a different name."

"Maybe it's spelled funny."

"How many ways are there to spell 'wind'? No, I'm sure I have the whole name wrong. Thanks anyway for your help."

"It's what I'm here for."

Rainie left the building and went back to her car. Maybe Lucas really did own that land. Even though she might have better luck in buying it from a corporation, she almost hoped it was his. Dealing with him, even as stubborn as he pretended to be, would be more fun than trying to negotiate with some stuffy corporate executive. But who was she trying to kid? Getting the use of his land had been a priority at one point, but Lucas himself, was the real prize.

As she turned onto the highway that led back to her ranch, she was thinking about how easily she had overcome his original demands that she stay away. Obviously he hadn't meant to enforce the ban, and he seemed to be enjoying her company. In fact, he had almost kissed her, and that meant he wasn't entirely as locked in to the solitary life as he pretended. But then she did wonder why he had drawn back. Shyness? That seemed possible. A gregarious, outgoing person would hardly choose to live in such an isolated cabin. Yes, he must be shy. Rainie smiled. At one time she, too, had been shy, and she'd hated being that way. She had every intention of helping him overcome that. Even a shy man could be wooed, if one didn't rush things.

A glance at the clock in her car told her she'd have to shower and change clothes in a hurry so she wouldn't be late to Marla's wedding shower.

BY MIDAFTERNOON the next day, a light rain was falling. Rainie had been out in all sorts of weather with her horses, so she didn't really mind. Unless rain was coming down in buckets, with lightning in the vicinity, she paid it no heed. Marla's wedding shower the night before had left her feeling pensive, for throughout the evening she had fantasized what it would be like if she and Lucas were in the place of Marla and Bob. Then she'd had to go home alone.

However the melancholy was gone when she'd awakened, and by working faster than usual, she had finished her daily chores hours early and had already showered, changed clothes, and saddled India for the ride up the mountain to Lucas's cabin and their supper date.

She double-checked to be sure she had her waterproof camera bag, which contained a selection of books she thought Lucas would enjoy, and after mounting her horse, she arranged her poncho so that her legs and the saddle were covered. Pulling the hood up over her hair, she headed out of the barn. As she passed through the doors, she unhooked the heavy utility flashlight from its place by the door, and looped it over the saddle horn.

As soon as India was out in the rain, he flattened his ears in protest, but she headed him up the mountain anyway. Because of the heavy cloud cover, the woods were dark and the meadows seemed shrouded in a silvery gauze from the fine misting rain. On days like this, the spring flowers took on a surrealistic glow and the forest was magical.

As usual, Lucas came out on the porch to greet her as soon as she entered the clearing. "Hi," she called out cheerfully.

"You came." He sounded amazed.

"You asked me to come for supper. Remember?" She looked up at him in confusion. "Do I have the wrong night?"

"No, but it's raining."

"Don't you eat when it rains? I do."

"I didn't think you'd come up in weather like this."

Rainie looked around as if to see what he meant. "It's barely sprinkling." She looked back at him. "Is it okay if I put India in your barn? I don't want to leave him tied in the rain."

He paused, then said, "Sure." He came down the steps and preceded her across to the barn. At the door he hesitated again, then opened it for her. Parked in the central aisle was a cherry red '57 BelAir Chevy.

"Wow!" Rainie said in wonder as she dismounted. "Would you look at that! Whose car is this?"

"Mine. You can put your horse in this stall. I'm afraid I don't have any feed or hay to give him."

"That's okay. I'll feed him when I get home." She was still studying the sleek lines of the car and its celebrated rear fender fins. "No wonder you don't worry about driving after groceries. I love classic cars. Did you buy it recently? No, I'll bet it belonged to your parents, right? You sure have kept it in good condition."

"I'll unsaddle your horse." He lifted the stirrup over the saddle and unfastened the leather cinch strap. "I don't have a curry comb, either."

She picked up a rag from a bench. "I'll dry him off with this, if you don't mind."

He nodded.

When she had India settled, she fastened the stall gate and went back to the car. Bending over and looking through the window, she said, "White leather seats? No, I guess they're imitation, aren't they? This is beautiful!"

"Come on back to the house. Dinner is almost ready."

He seemed nervous and ill at ease, so Rainie smiled to show him she was sure she could eat anything he could cook.

They went back through the rain to the porch, and as Rainie slipped the bulky poncho over her head, Lucas noticed that the jeans she was wearing were molded to her body and her frilly, white Western shirt, which was also close-fitting, was unbuttoned low enough to show a hint of cleavage. At her neck gleamed a thin gold chain. "Should I leave my poncho out here? I don't want to puddle your floor."

Lucas had been unconsciously staring down at her trim figure, but when she spoke, he abruptly met her eyes. Had he thought she was merely pretty? She was beautiful. In the porch light he could see diamonds of raindrops clinging to the long lashes surrounding her navy blue eyes. Her complexion was radiant, and her lips full and sensual. For a moment he indulged himself in the fantasy of kissing each of the raindrops on her cheeks, her chin and her lips. Self-consciously he shoved his hands into his pockets. "Just hang your poncho on one of the pegs out here."

He pushed open the door and stood back for her to enter. As she reached up to hang her poncho where he'd indicated, he couldn't help but notice how her blouse outlined her breasts and that her nipples were erect. Her hair, hanging loose about her shoulders, looked like fine, dark silk. She was so small, her head would fit easily under his chin. When she smiled at him, he felt his heart skip a beat in response.

Rainie stepped into the cabin and sighed with delight. Far from being the messy bachelor's lair he had intimated it would be, the place was scrubbed and as orderly as her own house. While there were no feminine touches or even curtains at the windows, the furniture looked comfortable and a brightly colored rag rug covered the wood floor. A low fire crackled on the hearth, and she was reminded that the cabin had no central heat. The delicious aroma of stew filled the air.

"I wasn't sure you'd come," he repeated. "All I cooked was stew."

"I love stew. Especially on a night like this." She went to the counter that divided the kitchen from the rest of the room. "How do you manage without a refrigerator?"

"That's easy. I buy canned food. I'm not much of a cook and I don't entertain."

She glanced at him, her curiosity piqued by his choice of words. She would have expected a mountain man to think in terms of having company, not entertaining. Something didn't ring true again, but she chose to overlook it as she had the other seeming inconsistencies.

"So I'm afraid we're just having canned stew and crackers. I'll understand, if you'd rather not stay."

"Are you trying to get rid of me? All I'm trying to do is be your friend." She had a great deal more in mind, but as shy as he was, she had to take this a little at a time.

Lucas felt a twinge of embarrassment. He was being rude and that was a trait he would have said didn't even belong to him. "I'm sorry. It's only that my privacy is very important, and I'm not looking for any commitments."

"Neither am I," she lied. "All I had in mind was sitting down with a friend and eating canned stew and crackers."

He realized they were still standing. "Have a seat. The stew is already hot."

"Thank you," she said graciously.

When she took her place at the scarred table, Lucas put a place mat and a paper napkin in front of her. His place mat was red and white checked; hers was blue with a parade of ducks.

"Nothing matches," he said apologetically. "I just have odds and ends here."

"That's fine." She watched him as he ladled a generous helping of stew, first into a white enameled bowl, then into a blue one with white flecks. He gave her the blue one. "Thanks. It goes with the ducks." She grinned disarmingly.

He sat opposite her and put his paper napkin in his lap. "You're the only woman I know who would ride a horse up a mountain in the rain to eat canned stew."

"Am I? Working with my horses the way I do, I don't notice the weather unless it's really bad." As she unexpectedly jumped up and went to the door, he stared after her. "I almost forgot." She unhooked the camera bag from beneath the poncho and brought it inside. Returning to the table she said, "I brought you these."

"More sandwiches?"

"Books."

Lucas hesitated. "I'm really not much of a mystery fan."

"That's okay because I didn't bring any mysteries. Go ahead. Look at them." She tasted the stew as he unzipped the bag. "This is good. Spicy, just the way I like it."

He took out three books, and when he read the title of the last one he almost choked. "You read Jordan Lane?" he asked.

"He's one of my favorites. That's one of his newest books, and I thought you might not have read it."

Lucas cautiously turned the book over and saw his own portrait—clean-shaven, short-haired, and suit-bedecked—

smiling back at him. He was glad he hadn't followed his editor's advice to update his publicity photo to show his beard. Glancing up, he was relieved that Rainie was paying more attention to her bowl of stew than she was to his reaction. He turned the book right-side up and put it back in the bag. "I've read this one."

"You've read *Wildfire*? What did you think of it?"

"What did you think?" he hedged.

"I like all of Jordan Lane's books, but I felt the ending was a little weak in this one."

He frowned. "Weak? What do you mean weak?"

"If I were the heroine in that book, I'd have reacted differently. She should have thought of her pregnancy as a future baby, not a medical condition. That would change the entire ending."

"But this heroine was a professional woman! The head of her own company! She made multimillion-dollar decisions every day."

Rainie shrugged. "She's still a woman."

A growling sound rumbled from Lucas's chest.

"And I wondered how she knew the company's saboteur was her business partner. It could just as easily have been her ex-husband from the clues that were given."

"Impossible! Her ex-husband didn't think that way at all. If anything, it was too obvious that her business partner was to blame."

"You think so? Maybe I missed something. Like I said, I thought the ending was weak. *Evening Song* is my favorite."

Grudgingly Lucas nodded. "It was on the *New York Times'* list longer than any of the others."

"How do you know that?"

He looked away. "I guess I read it somewhere."

Rainie reached for a cracker as she said, "I wonder what it's like to be a writer and live such a glamorous life."

"If writers lived like their characters do, they wouldn't have time to write books."

She tilted her head to one side as she considered his words. "You know, I never thought of that."

Lucas realized the subject could be too revealing for comfort, so he asked, "How did you get the name Rainie?"

"My parents were of the generation which named its babies things like Freedom and Sunshine and . . . Rainie. They met in college when they were doing a sit-in to protest women's inequality. Mom said I was born on a rainy day, so that's what they named me, rain being a sign of growth and plenty and so forth."

"It's unusual. I like it."

"My brothers are just glad they were named after family members and not a weather condition or a virtue. My middle name is Elizabeth, but I never use it. Rainie suits me, I think."

"I think so, too. You're certainly unpredictable."

"Thank you."

She watched as he finished his bowl of stew and offered her seconds, which she declined. He was so handsome she was surprised no woman had snatched him up, hermit or no hermit. And he was intelligent. When they had discussed that book, he had seemed almost fervent in his opinion.

As he dipped stew into his bowl, she said, "I'm surprised you've never been married."

"What makes you assume that?"

"Have you?"

"As a matter of fact, I was. I've been divorced over a year now."

Rainie looked around the room. "She must have taken the curtains with her when she left."

Lucas smiled, but didn't answer.

"Married life didn't seem to agree with me, either."

"That surprises me. I would have said you aren't cut out to be a loner."

"I'm not, but I don't have the patience to be a housewife, either. That was the hardest job I ever had. Training horses is less physically taxing. I must have buffed a thousand square acres of floors and washed a mountain of dishes in those eight years."

"Eight? Mine only lasted five."

Rainie studied him for a long moment before speaking. "I guess she got lonely up here. Some people need more company than others."

"Loneliness wasn't one of the complaints she mentioned."

Again she indulged herself in the fantasy of what it would be like to be his wife, and she blushed. With his intensity about something as trivial as a book, he would probably be a passionate husband.

"Why are you blushing?"

"I was just thinking that I wouldn't have complained if I had been her."

Lucas swallowed hastily to keep from choking. Had she meant that the way it had sounded?

After the meal Rainie insisted on drying the dishes while Lucas washed. As she wiped the bowls dry, she marveled that such a simple chore could feel so intimate. He had rolled his shirtsleeves up to his elbows, and the hot, soapy water left a film of bubbles over his bare forearms. His black hair fell over his forehead as he bent toward the sink.

When he handed her the two spoons, their fingers touched and Rainie felt the sensation all the way to her middle. Startled, she raised her eyes to find he was looking down at her with the same surprise she felt. Hastily she averted her eyes and took the spoons, drying them more vigorously than was necessary. Lucas plunged his hands back into the soapy water, obviously renewing his focus on the job at hand.

After passing the pot through the rinse water, he handed it to Rainie, and she dried it with efficient swipes of the soft cloth. The pot was still warm from the dishwater. "Where does this go?"

"Here." He automatically reached past her to a cabinet, and she found herself almost in his arms. Again their eyes met and this time they were more reluctant to look away.

She gazed into his dark eyes and saw the struggle within him not to kiss her. Now that she knew he had been married and divorced, she wondered if that was why he wanted to keep his distance. Some divorces were as scarring as abuse. Maybe he still had bruises on his ego. She waited to see what he would do.

After a long minute he stepped back and silently opened the cabinet door. She could tell he was shaken. Maybe even as shaken as she was.

"Dessert!" he said with forced cheerfulness as he grabbed up an old cracker tin. "Cookies."

They sat on the couch in front of the fire, the tin box of cookies between them as if it were a bundling board. The cookies were store-bought, but it was a brand that brought back childhood memories for Rainie. Lucas propped his feet on the battered coffee table, and Rainie slipped her feet out of her shoes and did the same. The fire pleasantly warmed the soles of her feet, and she wiggled her toes in response.

"You have small feet." His observation surprised her.

"I do?" She lifted her outstretched leg and turned her foot about experimentally.

"They're nice."

She laughed. "You finally say something nice to me, and it's a compliment about my feet?"

"I've said other things to you that were nice."

"Name one."

"I've said you have beautiful eyes."

She stared at him in disbelief. "No, you didn't."

"I must have."

"I would have remembered that."

He looked at her as if he were memorizing every feature of her face. "You have beautiful eyes."

"So do you."

He hastily held up the tin. "Have another cookie?"

Automatically she reached in and took two as their eyes met. More was going on here than their words implied. She offered him one of them. "You look like you could use one, too."

"Thanks."

They went back to watching the fire in silence, but Rainie couldn't stop the quickening of her pulse. His nearness was almost overwhelming her. She could feel tension emanating from him as if he were struggling as hard as she was to appear detached.

"I guess we could work out some agreement on you using my land," he said, breaking the awkward silence. "There's no sense in it lying fallow."

"I'd stay out of your way," she promised. "If I could fence off the upper part, you'd never see any of my horses. I can have Billy and Oscar clear a road farther to the west beyond that grove of pines so it won't be in sight of the cabin."

"I guess I'd still see you once in a while. Right?"

"Oh, sure. If you want to. I don't want to be a pest."

"No?" he asked with a laugh. "Then why didn't you clear out the first time I told you to?"

"You didn't mean it."

"I didn't?"

"You probably thought you did, but your eyes looked lonely."

"No, they didn't."

"Yes, they did."

"Look, Rainie, I can't go into all the details, but I need my privacy."

"Can you go into a few of them?"

"You said it yourself. I'm a hermit and hermits have to be alone or they aren't hermits. Okay?"

"I think it's your divorce."

"I beg your pardon?"

"You must have been hurt so badly that you have trouble trusting a woman now."

"That's it. You guessed it. I've never met anyone as astute as you are. So . . . will you let me go on about my business of being a recluse?"

"No."

"What?"

"How can I let you pine away up here now that we're friends?"

"How did we get to be friends all of a sudden?"

"Well, I don't ride a horse up a mountain on a rainy night to eat canned stew with someone who is not a friend. I thought we had already established that."

"I'll send a few cans of stew home with you and we'll make a pact to eat it on Tuesdays and Thursdays, you at your house and me at mine."

"That's sad."

"What's sad?"

"That she hurt you so badly. Lucas, you just have to put that behind you, and not let it matter so much."

He tried to control his exasperation. "It *doesn't* matter. I didn't contest the divorce. My heart isn't broken!"

To his amazement he saw pity darken her eyes. "I understand."

"No, you don't!"

"Lucas, I couldn't forgive myself if I let you think all women would shrug you off so easily. So I'm going to be your friend."

"Don't do me any favors, Rainie."

She smiled, and the dimple appeared in her chin. "You don't have to thank me."

Before he knew what she was going to do, she leaned over and kissed him. "I want to be your friend," she said softly.

Lucas was surprised at the spontaneity of her gesture. She started to draw back, but he put his arms around her, holding her close. From this distance he could see the depths of her soul in her dark blue eyes and feel the warmth of her slender body. She was soft and curvaceous, but firm with muscle tone. All of Rainie seemed to be a contradiction. He found her irresistible. Slowly he drew her nearer.

Her lips were soft and warm against his and her breath was sweet. As he moved his mouth over hers, her lips parted. Lucas felt his desire begin to mount. He wasn't the only one who was lonely. Her kiss told him that.

She swayed closer and he wrapped one arm about her while threading his other hand through her hair. Rainie had glorious hair—thick and sleek and as sweet-smelling as a spring shower. It glided through his fingers like silk.

Rainie put her arms around his neck and returned his kiss with an eagerness that took Lucas's breath away. He tasted the softness of her inner lips and her tongue caressed his tongue intimately.

Lucas groaned softly in his effort to control himself. He wanted her, and he knew she wouldn't object. His hand circled her rib cage to cover her breast. It was soft and firm like the rest of her and her nipple was already pouting for his attention. Lucas unsnapped the two upper fasteners of her blouse and slipped his hand inside. Her bra was made of lacy silk and did nothing to conceal the shape of her breast from his questing fingers. He ran his fingertips between the fabric and her warm skin. Rainie murmured with desire.

He lowered his head to trail kisses from her moist lips down her chin and throat as he eased her back onto the cushions. Lucas brushed aside the blouse and gazed at her breasts in the nearly transparent bra, before lowering his head to nuzzle at one nipple.

Rainie arched toward him and Lucas realized where this was heading and with what speed. He wanted her so much, he ached, but he knew Rainie's impulsiveness. He didn't want to do anything she might regret tomorrow.

Lucas needed all his willpower to stroke her breasts one last time, then to pull her blouse back over them. Rainie looked at him in surprise. "I don't want to rush into this," he said, his voice husky with repressed emotion. "Tomorrow you might not feel the same way about me that you do right now."

"Or maybe I would." Her voice sounded breathless and a bit disappointed.

"Rainie, we can't do whatever we please without any thoughts of the consequences. We're neighbors and we just agreed to a business deal about pasture rights. Even if you should decide tomorrow you never want to see me again, it would be difficult. We can't simply go our own ways and never see each other again."

She was silent. She sat up and began refastening her blouse.

"I didn't mean to hurt your feelings or to embarrass you."

"I'm not. I'm just thinking." She kept her face turned away.

"Rainie," he said as he gently pulled her face around so their eyes could meet. "It's not that I don't want you."

She gazed deep into his eyes, as if she were trying to read his thoughts. At last she nodded. "I have to be going."

Lucas made no effort to stop her. If she stayed, he wasn't all that sure he could control his desire for her. This was for the best, he told himself. But he was regretting it far more than he had thought he would.

She stood up and went to the door. "I'm still going to be your friend."

He turned to look at her, but she had stepped out into the misty night. Lucas missed her already.

5

LUCAS LAY AWAKE most of the night. The intimacy he and Rainie had shared had affected him deeply, and he was completely at a loss as to what to do about her.

She was so cheerful and independent, yet he sensed a vulnerable core that would scar easily. He couldn't make love to Rainie for the few weeks he would be here and then just walk away. Such cavalier treatment might hurt her worse than her broken marriage had. And he wasn't sure he would be able to leave her at all, if they became lovers.

For some reason she touched his soul in a way no one else ever had. It wasn't simply that she had the wide-eyed innocence of someone who believes in fairies and in wishes on rainbows, or that she was delightfully unpredictable, or that she had more sex appeal in her compact body than any woman he'd ever known. Rainie had an aura about her that seemed to dovetail exactly with his own. Whenever he saw her, it was as if he were seeing her for the first time, and yet, it was as though he'd always known her.

He stared up at the vee-grooved boards on his ceiling, trying to decide what to do about Rainie Sheenan. Had it not been for his decision to stop, he was sure they would have made love. His body still ached to possess her, but he knew he had done the right thing. Aside from the scar it might have left on Rainie's spirit, there were other complications.

Lucas had learned the hard way that it wasn't wise to become lovers with someone who couldn't be avoided after the affair was over. Rainie was his neighbor, and he had agreed to let her use his pastures. Even though he'd return home and their communication would be from a distance, any former intimacy could make things decidedly uncomfortable. And as he had no intention of ever selling his family land, and she seemed equally settled on the Rainbow Ranch, or whatever it was she had named it, their business arrangement might keep them in contact for years to come.

Then there was his true identity to further muddy the waters. She knew him by his real name—the one he rarely used on anything but legal documents. Even close friends called him Jordan, because he was known all over the world as Jordan Lane. At times he felt as if Jordan Lane had a life separate and apart from him.

Reporters and publicity agents had touted the famous author as a playboy who hobnobbed with royalty aboard princely yachts and entertained in lavish penthouses. Lucas wasn't like that at all. True, he knew some of the minor royal families and he had a number of friends who happened to be wealthy, but he never thought of himself as anything but Lucas Dalton. Women, however, believed implicitly in Jordan Lane.

He was certain that if he told Rainie who he really was it would alter their relationship. She would either draw back and insist he take his place on a pedestal, or she would forget Lucas and love the mythical Jordan. It had happened to him too many times before.

By dawn he gave up trying to sleep and went into the small room he had set up as an office. His writer's block was there waiting for him, the blank page on the typewriter relentlessly reminding him of its existence. Lucas drew another black line through the previous day's date on his calendar. Another day was gone; the deadline was another day nearer.

Once more he read through the synopsis for his novel, hoping this time his creative muse would provide the inspiration he needed.

RAINIE GRACEFULLY POSTED across her arena on the horse she was exercising, rising from the English saddle and returning to it in rhythm with the horse's trot, her full attention fixed on the task at hand. With a touch of her knees, she commanded the horse to change leads. He was performing flawlessly.

The sound of a car door slamming broke her concentration, and she glanced up to see Tom Hanford crossing from her drive to the exercise arena. She smiled a greeting, but had the horse finish his paces before she rode him over to speak with the sheriff.

"That's a beauty," Hanford said. "He's a far cry from your herd of scarecrows."

"He should be. January was named Best in Show his last three times out. He's making quite a name for himself. I'll probably keep him another year, then sell him. By then he'll probably be just past his peak."

Hanford nodded as if he knew all about showing horses. "Once they reach their peak is the time to sell. They bring top dollar then."

Rainie smiled.

Hanford shifted his weight, and the sun glinted off his badge. "I came out here on official business," he said, deepening his tone to a level he must have thought sounded more authoritative.

"Oh? Have you found some reason to arrest Fredricks again?"

"No, but I'm still keeping an eye on him. This is about a kidnapping."

Rainie shaded the sun from her eyes with her hand and frowned at the sheriff. "A kidnapping? There's a child missing in Lupine?"

"No, no, nothing like that. This is something that came in over the wire. That writer fellow, Jordan Lane, is missing."

Rainie's mouth dropped open. "You're kidding! Jordan Lane is one of my favorite authors! But what does that have to do with Lupine?"

"Well, you know he lives over in Memphis."

"He does? I had no idea. I assumed he lived in New York or someplace like that."

"Nope. He's lived in Memphis for years. Seems his car was seen in Millsburg, heading this way. There's word of a stranger in Roan Oak. I talked to the Roan Oak sheriff this morning—he's a friend of mine—and got a description."

"There must be strangers coming and going all the time. The highway goes right through there."

"Yeah, I thought of that, but Joe Odom, he's the sheriff over there, says this stranger that's been hanging around first showed up about the time Lane went missing. He wasn't driving Lane's car, but a kidnapper would have hidden that one so he couldn't be traced by it. Wears faded jeans and flannel shirts or old sweatshirts mostly."

"The sheriff over there seems to be keeping as close an eye on things as you do."

"Well, you have to these days. Generally it's pretty quiet around here, but things can get out of hand real quick, if you don't stay on top of them. You see a stranger once, you don't think much of it. But you see him again, and you start getting suspicious. Same's true of Sheriff Odom. You see, that's what drew the sheriff's attention. This stranger comes in and buys supplies and leaves again without saying more than a word or two to anybody. A week or two later, he's back again. Been there two or three times now. The man that owns the grocery said he acts like he doesn't want anybody to get to know him."

"Maybe he moved here and just isn't very friendly."

"Not likely. Roan Oak's not much bigger than Lupine. I'll bet neither town has more than one family move in over a year's time."

"What does he look like?"

"Joe says he's about six foot or taller, dark hair, thin, has a beard."

"That description fits a large part of the male population of Roan Oak."

"I know. It's like he was trying to blend in and not be noticed. Joe says he has a sneaky way of moving and doesn't make eye contact very often with anybody."

"That does sound rather suspicious."

"He says the man just gets whatever he came after and leaves. Won't even pass the time of day."

Rainie nodded. She was well aware that to the people who lived in the small mountain towns around Lupine, a newcomer's failure to be friendly was almost considered a crime, yet these same people preferred to stay aloof from anyone new until he proved to be one of them. Rainie had experienced this paradox herself.

"So I'm going around town asking if anyone has seen anything odd or met up with any strangers," the sheriff continued.

"Not me. I met a man named Lucas Dalton last week, but he's a local, a mountain man."

"I don't know any Daltons."

"He shops in Roan Oak. He's not a stranger, though, because he was born right there in his cabin and so were his ancestors."

"Next time you see him, you might warn him to be on the lookout for strangers."

Rainie smiled. "Where Lucas lives, no one would be apt to go. He's a bit of a hermit. I ran across him by accident myself while I was trying to catch one of my new horses that had run onto the land that backs up to my place."

"You ought to be careful riding around by yourself. Could be dangerous."

"What makes you think the kidnappers would be around here?"

"Lupine and Roan Oak are in a straight line with Millsburg and Memphis. If I was going to hide out and wait for ransom to be paid, I'd find myself a little town like Roan Oak, where I thought the sheriff and locals wouldn't know about what I had done, and I'd sit back and hole up."

"They're asking a ransom?"

"Not yet. His family is waiting to be contacted."

"I never thought of Jordan Lane as having parents. From all I've heard, I just assumed he emerged from a party fully grown."

"I don't know a thing about them, not even whether 'family' means parents or a wife and kids. Just that no ransom has been demanded as yet."

"I sure never pictured him with a wife and children, either."

"I guess whoever took him figures to make a bundle from it. I hear tell he's rich as a crocus."

Rainie fought back the urge to grin at the sheriff's botched simile, and refrained from pointing out his mistake. Tom Hanford was one of those people who was never wrong. "That's really a shame. I just read his latest book a few weeks ago."

"I hear he's a good writer. Never read one of them myself."

"He's terrific. But this one had a weak ending, I thought."

Tom nodded. "Well, I've got to be moving on. You keep an eye out, you hear? Anything suspicious, anything at all, you give me a call."

"I will."

She rode the horse to the barn, and after unsaddling him, she brushed his rich, bay coat until it was shining, then turned him onto the exercise wheel to cool him down slowly.

Next on her daily routine was an inspection of the horses she was trying to save. As she leaned on the feed lot fence, she studied the motley assortment of horses. So far they were all alive, even the old sorrel mare. The buckskin colt was already showing some improvement, and it wouldn't be long before he'd have enough stamina to lead her on a genuine chase if he got loose again. He had become pretty special to her because it was almost as though he had led her to Lucas.

All six of the horses were becoming accustomed to her, though none except the colt was trusting enough as yet to come to her on his own. She felt that in time that trust would develop, but then some horses were never easy to catch. Her own horse, Blaze, was an example of that, and Blaze had never been mistreated in his entire life. It wasn't that he didn't trust her, but rather he was playing hard to get. It was sort of a game with him, not unlike the behavior of a certain mountain man.

But unlike horses, which tended to copy the rebellious actions of one of their group, Lucas was a man, who had his own reasons for not wanting others close to him, whatever those reasons might be. The night before, she had wanted to make love with him, but he had held back as if he didn't trust his own feelings. She had not encouraged him to continue because he was already reticent about his relationship with her and she didn't want to rush things. She was sure she could develop trust with her new horses, but could she do the same with Lucas? Only time would tell.

She bent over and slipped her body between the rails of the fence. At once the horses became uneasy and moved to the far corner. With her hands stuffed in her back pockets, Rainie walked slowly toward them. As the horses moved to keep their distance, she watched the chestnut mare that was heavy with foal.

True, the animal was so thin that she might look as if her unborn colt was larger than it really was, but Rainie's practiced eye told her the horse was nearer to term than the vet had thought. Bob had been out recently, and she was reluctant to call him back for another look so soon. With his wedding and honeymoon so imminent, Bob was trying to get all his loose ends tied up so he and Marla could be gone for a few days.

Rainie studied the way the mare moved and how she carried herself, but still was unsure. She could be wrong. Bob was the vet, and he thought the mare would wait another three weeks or so. If anything, Rainie decided, she ought to be worried about the sorrel mare. She hadn't improved a bit and still might not pull out of it.

After a few more minutes Rainie went in search of Billy and Oscar and told them what she wanted them to do that afternoon. At times she wondered why she bothered; Oscar knew as much about ranching as she did, and Billy seemed to have a natural instinct for training horses. Thanks to the three of them, the ranch had become profitable in a remarkably short time.

After a quick lunch Rainie went to the barn and saddled India and a tall horse named Red. This time she and Lucas would ride while they talked and avoid, for the time being, the intimacy that seemed to make him so uncomfortable. Perhaps this would help build his trust in her and in himself. Riding India and leading the other horse, she started up the mountain. In her anticipation of seeing Lucas, she forgot all about her conversation with Tom Hanford.

This time she was all the way across the porch and knocking on the door before he knew she was there. From the interior of the cabin she heard a door slam and hurried footsteps as if he were clearing something out of sight and then another slamming door. The pace of Lucas's footsteps slowed as he crossed the room to the front door. *How sweet*, she thought, *he's straightening up the room to impress me.* He opened the door, but his body blocked her view of the room.

"Your reflexes are slowing down," she observed as her eyes skimmed his magnificent physique from head to foot. "You usually meet me on the porch."

"What are you doing here?" He was almost out of breath. "After you left so abruptly last night, I wasn't sure you'd be back."

"I told you I was still going to be your friend, and it's such a lovely day, I thought we might go for a ride. See? I brought you a horse."

"You have to stop coming up here without giving me any warning."

"Don't worry about me seeing your place in a mess. I know bachelors are notoriously poor housekeepers. It doesn't matter. Besides, how can I call and tell you I'm coming when you have no phone?"

"You could wait until you're invited."

"Lucas, if I stood on such ceremony as that, I would never have come up here the second time, now would I? You know how shy you are." She smiled and added, "Aren't you going to ask me in?"

"No." He came outside and closed the door firmly behind him.

He was playing the same game Blaze often did. *Cajole me and I'll come, but I won't make it easy.* Rainie nodded toward the extra horse. "His name is Red, and he came with the farm. I'm afraid he isn't as smooth gaited as my saddle horses, but he's very gentle. I thought you might be more comfortable with him."

"I know how to ride," he said testily.

"Of course, you do." She patted his arm to show she would accept him whether he really did or not. "Are you ready to go?"

"If I say no, will you leave?"

"No."

Lucas sighed. "Then let's go." All day he had tried unsuccessfully to write, but he'd been able to think only about what it would have been like to make love with Rainie. Both issues had been frustrating him and had left him tense. He was truly pleased that she had come, but was at odds with himself as to how to deal with her.

"I wouldn't impose like this if I thought I was interrupting anything," she said as she mounted India. "But since you don't seem to have anything else to do, I thought we might as well take advantage of the good weather. Let's ride to the upper meadow, and I'll explain what I have in mind for a barn."

She watched as he looped the reins over Red's head and held them and the saddle horn in his left hand as he swung into the saddle. Perhaps, she thought, he really did know how to ride. Certainly he seemed at home with the animal.

At a leisurely pace they rode up the weed-choked road that wound around the side of the mountain. The horses had no difficulty picking their way, as the road had apparently been built wide enough to accommodate wagons.

"Why was this road cut through here, I wonder?" she asked as she gazed at the vista of blue hills through a break in the trees. "It doesn't seem to go anywhere."

"My grandmother told me there was once another cabin up in the crest. That family and mine intermarried, and because the cabin I'm in is larger, the newlyweds lived in it. Eventually the people in the one above here either moved on or died, and the cabin ultimately fell down. Mine is in a more sheltered location and has always been lived in and cared for, so it's in sound shape."

"It's funny about houses, isn't it," she mused. "They fall apart if they aren't lived in. It's almost as if they need to have people and life inside their walls."

"I've noticed that, too, but I can't explain it. Maybe people do more automatic upkeep than they realize."

"Do you know where the cabin used to stand?"

"I haven't been up here in years, but I can find it."

She let him ride slightly ahead so she could watch him without him knowing she did so. He sat easily in the saddle and was firm but gentle with the horse. She had chosen Red not only because of his even temperament, but because he didn't have a tender mouth. Now she saw her precautions had been unnecessary because Lucas wasn't one to jerk or haul on a horse. Her estimation of him soared. Rainie had always thought she could tell more about a person by the way he reacted to animals than in any other way.

After reaching the top of the mountain, Lucas guided them into a clearing. "This it it. There used to be a fence about halfway between here and my cabin," he told her. "It took in all three meadows. The people who used to live here cleared quite a bit of land, and I wouldn't object if you have your men cut out the undergrowth. Just enough so grass will grow, but not enough to scalp it. Leave the larger trees."

"Naturally. They make windbreaks for the winter." He led her to the opposite edge of the clearing and pointed. "The cabin used to sit there. See the rocks that supported it and what's left of the chimney?"

Rainie dismounted and tied her horse to a tree before walking to the old foundation. It had been a small cabin, she noticed. Probably not as large as the main room of Lucas's. Squat, flat stones had been stacked to support the four corners and more were stacked amid a pile of rubble. The logs had long since rotted away, and the ground was soft and loamy with their remains.

"Think what it must have been like to settle here," she said dreamily. "They would have had to be completely self-sufficient—Lupine and Roan Oak wouldn't have been here then. How lonely it must have been."

"I imagine they had so much work to do that there wasn't much time for loneliness. It's hard to imagine a whole family living in such a small space, though."

Rainie looked at him in surprise. She had assumed he and his parents and probably at least one grandparent had lived together in his cabin. He was gazing off into the distance, as if his mind was on the long-vanished family.

"What a view they had! My cabin is surrounded by woods, but from here you can see to forever and back again."

Rainie had the déjà vu sensation of having read that phrase somewhere, but she ignored it. "I'll bet the wife was so proud of this house. She probably planted flowers around it and made curtains for the windows."

"The windows would have had wooden shutters, too. With civilization so far away, they would have had to be leery of Indian attacks."

"I thought the Indians around here were friendly."

"We know now they were, but in the early 1800s they didn't know that yet. And there were probably bands of outlaws among the Indians that weren't friendly, whether it was tribal policy or not."

"True." She stood within the foundation and gazed out over the silent miles of mountains. "In the winter this cabin must have felt isolated indeed."

"It was. My own cabin would be snowed in fairly early and it's more protected than this one."

What an odd way to put it, she thought. Almost as if he assumed it, but hadn't witnessed it firsthand. "How do you get food and supplies in the winter?"

"I manage."

He walked over to an area several yards away. "I think the original barn was here, but if I were you, I'd put the barn in the lower meadow and use this one for grazing."

"I agree. Why do you suppose they built here in such an exposed spot?"

He shrugged. "Just because they were pioneers doesn't mean they knew what they were doing. Maybe they settled here as a young couple—possibly still in their teens—and thought the view was pretty. By the time bad weather rolled around, they might have already built the house and barn. Moving to a more sheltered area and starting over might have seemed to be more trouble than it was worth."

"I never thought of inept pioneers. Yet there must have been some," she admitted.

"Most historical periods sound romantic and picturesque to people who don't have to live in them."

"That's very profound."

"It's only logical. We like to think of them as times when families were closer and work was shared willingly—corn husking and quilting bees and that sort of thing. But it was also a time when the loss of a sewing needle could be a small catastrophe, and when a cut with a rusty nail or simple disease by today's standards could be fatal."

Rainie stared at him, curious at his insight.

"We tend to overlook the lack of sanitation and the basic ignorance. Not all the pioneers left civilization because they had a dream. Some left because no one would hire them, or because they were one step ahead of the law, or because they were social outcasts."

"You continually amaze me. I never thought of any of this."

Lucas clamped his mouth shut, realizing he had been talking too freely. None of this would have occurred to him, either, if he hadn't done research in order to write the outline that was causing his writer's block.

"I guess with no television you have more time to think than most people," Rainie said.

"That's it," he said with a grin, hoping he sounded convincing. "I have lots and lots of time."

She broke a twig off a nearby tree and twirled it between her thumb and forefinger. "Don't you get bored? I couldn't survive without contact with people." She turned her head and fixed her gaze on him, and the intimacy of his penetrating stare was unsettling.

"Lately, I've had contact almost every day."

"You mean me? I'm only being friendly." The corners of her mouth turned up in a most tantalizing way. Didn't she know what she was doing to him? She called it being friendly, but to him it was provocative—much more provocative than he was sure he could cope with. When she looked at him this way, it was all he could do to control himself. She was seldom out of his mind. Lucas found himself thinking about her dozens of times each day, wishing he could enfold her in his arms and make love with her for hours on end. She was still watching him, waiting for his reply, but he couldn't say what he was thinking. He had no time for this. He had a novel to write. Maybe when he was through . . . Tightening his jaw to keep his emotions out of his voice, he responded, "All the same, you've turned my world inside out."

To Rainie's ears, the tenseness of his words sounded like resentment. "I didn't mean to be a pest." She had tried hard to avoid the intimacy that seemed to have upset him the night before. She had even resisted the temptation to reach out and touch him when they were close and had refrained from anything even remotely flirtatious. That had been difficult to do. Maybe she'd mistaken his shyness as caring for her, but shy. But what about his passion of the night before? Had she misread that, too? "Are you saying you really meant it when you told me to go away and not come back?" Embarrassment washed over her. How could she have been so dense?

"Rainie, I—"

"I'm sorry that I turned your world inside out," she said with all the dignity she could muster as she struggled not to let tears shake her voice. "All I wanted was a friend and a pasture. I can find both somewhere else." She turned on her heel and walked hurriedly toward her horse.

"Wait a minute!"

"You can return Red whenever you please, or better yet, I'll send Billy to get him. Goodbye, Lucas." She fumbled untying India's reins and was groping for the stirrup when he caught her arm and turned her around.

"You're crying!"

"I am not!" She blinked her tear-filled eyes and tried to focus on him.

"Rainie, listen to me." He gently took the reins from her hands and retied the horse. "You go off on tangents without ever checking to see if they're valid or not."

"You said—"

"I know what I said. And the first few times I saw you, I meant to chase you off."

"Well, it finally worked. I'm going."

He tightened his grip on her wrist to keep her in front of him. "That's not what I meant this time."

"I don't believe you."

"Damn it, Rainie, you're enough to try the patience of a saint. Now quit pulling away and listen to me."

Reluctantly she stopped struggling, but she continued to frown up at him.

"When I said you turned my world inside out, that was a compliment."

"Oh?" She tried to make her tone as aloof as possible.

"I meant you've become important to me. I find myself hoping you'll come to see me."

"If that's true, why don't you ever visit me?" she countered.

He drew a deep breath, as if he were considering how to answer this. "Because I can't encourage you. I shouldn't have done what I did last night. For one thing we're neighbors, and you're going to be using my land. You aren't someone I can avoid, if it doesn't work out."

Her frown deepened. "You can't be friends with only those certain people that you know you'll like forever. There aren't any guarantees, Lucas. Everybody knows that."

"What I'm feeling for you isn't exactly platonic," he quietly admitted.

Her pansy-blue eyes widened slightly. Did that mean he was spending as many sleepless night as she was?

"But for a lot of reasons—reasons I can't go into—I can't let myself get physically involved with you."

Her eyes softened in sympathy. That could explain why he had stopped short of making love with her. It wasn't that he didn't deeply care for her, but there was some sort of physical difficulty. "It's a medical problem?" she tactfully probed. "Maybe if you saw a doctor . . ."

He looked confused, then startled. "I didn't mean I'm impotent. Rainie, how do you keep your own thoughts sorted out when they jump around like that?"

"Then what did you mean?" Her mouth dropped open. "You can't mean you're . . . gay."

Lucas pulled her to him and pressed his lips over hers to prove to her that her latest assumption was absurd. At first Rainie was so surprised she pushed against him, but then she realized how right it felt to be in his arms. His lips were warm and firm, and intensely passionate. Her body fit against his as if it had been designed to match perfectly. His breath was sweet in her mouth.

Rainie put her arms around him and reached up, lacing her fingers in his thick hair. She felt the soft brush of his beard against her face as he cradled her head in his palm. His other arm pressed her hips against him, and she could feel his growing desire for her. She had never been kissed like this before. It wasn't that he was doing something unfamiliar; it was the way what he was doing affected her that was unique. The world seemed to rock beneath her, and she held on to Lucas as if he were the only reality.

When he finally lifted his head enough to gaze at her, she saw his eyes were dark and hot with longing. She was glad he still held her because she wasn't sure her legs would support her. At last she said, "I guess that was another wrong conclusion."

He laughed and held her so that her face was cuddled against his chest. She found she was laughing with him.

"Rainie," he said, "what am I going to do with you?"

"What do you want to do?"

Again he was serious; his eyes fixed on hers. He lifted his hand and stroked her cheek as if he wanted to remember and treasure this moment forever. "What I want to do, and what I must do are two different things."

"Do they have to be?"

After a long pause, he said, "Yes. At least they have to be for now. I have to think about this. To decide what to do."

"Your life sure is complicated for a man with no ties and no responsibilities," she observed wryly. "I thought that was supposed to be my line."

"Okay, then you tell me. What do you want to become of us? Where does our story go from here?"

Slowly she shook her head. "When you put it like that, I don't know how to answer."

"It's important that you realize this can't be something casual. Neither of us could handle that."

"How do you know? It's true about me—I don't ever have casual affairs. I haven't had any affairs at all. But how do you know that?"

"Let's just say my life has given me insight into people."

"I wouldn't have suspected that, since you so rarely see anyone."

He sighed and looked at her as if he wanted to explain but couldn't allow himself to do it. "Take my word for it. With us, it would never be a casual affair. I can tell you that for sure now."

She nodded. She didn't need a vast amount of experience to know he was right. In fact, she was now certain that she had fallen in love with him. The idea startled her. "I have to be going," she said abruptly. She hadn't intended to fall in love with him before she knew if those feelings would be mutual. But what about the statement she'd made to him that there were no guarantees? Wasn't it hypocritical of her not to want to fall in love with him until she knew he'd reciprocate? And what had he meant by saying that an affair between them wouldn't be casual for him? She had to have time to think.

They mounted and rode in silence down the mountain. Rainie could still feel his lips on hers and how his body had felt as she pressed against him. At his cabin they parted with only a few carefully chosen words, as if the ones they had shared in their embrace had been too meaningful to dilute with trivial conversation.

Only when Rainie was home again did she remember that she had not relayed the sheriff's warning to Lucas that he should be wary of strangers. But Jordan Lane and his kidnappers were so alien to Rainie's world that she had put it out of her mind. She had more than enough to sort out, what with her feelings of love for Lucas and his enigmatic reticence to become involved with her.

6

LUCAS OPENED his double barn doors and pale sunlight fell across the hood of his cherry-red Chevy. Taking a soft rag from the shelf, he dusted the car's exterior until it gleamed. This car was his pride and joy, and he much preferred it to the Mercedes he used for longer trips and autograph tours. He had tinkered with this old car until it ran like new. To look at it, a person would think it had just rolled off the show-room floor. During the weeks of his writer's block, he had groomed it to perfection.

He got in and fit his key into the ignition. The engine hummed to life. After allowing the car to thoroughly warm up, he turned the key off and got out. It wasn't good to let the car sit idle, but he had decided when he first got to the cabin that the classic design would draw too much attention to him in town, and thus he had been using his ancient Jeep for his trips into Roan Oak.

All the way to Roan Oak, his thoughts were on Rainie. He knew this was no mere physical desire that could be satiated and shelved. He was falling in love with her. This couldn't be allowed to happen. Lucas had enough on his mind with the encroaching deadline. Writer's block had already proved it-self a formidable opponent, without having love take over his thoughts, as well. He didn't have time to be in love! But how could he stop?

Roan Oak was not much different from many of the little mountain towns of the area that time had forgotten, with its narrow streets and buildings that dated back to the early days of the century. At one time some enterprising soul had installed parking meters down the main street, but now only the poles remained, looking like headless monoliths. But life wasn't absent in this sleepy little town. A few of the stores had planters out front filled with petunias, verbenas and pinks, which Lucas surmised were tended by the store owners' wives. Other storefronts sported wooden benches where colorful old men sat gossiping and swapping tales of their vanished youth.

Lucas parked in front of the building marked with the peeling, sun-bleached sign that proclaimed it to be the grocery of Witherspoon and Son. Like a relic of bygone days, the store had crates of onion sets and fruit on display in front of the windows.

Inside, Lucas was enveloped by the scents of fresh fruit, tomatoes and old wood. The aisles were barely wider than one shopping cart, but as Witherspoon's only had three carts there were seldom any traffic snarls. Unlike the crisp, freshly washed produce, some of the cans were dusty, looking as if they had resided on the shelves for a long time. Overhead hung an array of porcelain-coated washbasins and galvanized tin tubs and plastic buckets. Mops and brooms stood haphazard sentry duty in one corner. Feed bags were in another. Along the back was a meat counter where each selection was custom-sliced and wrapped while the customer waited.

Lucas enjoyed coming to this store. It was like slipping back into a comfortable past that he had never known firsthand. As a writer, he loved savoring the scents and sensations of new experiences, especially nostalgic ones. He came to the grocery store every two or three days as much for the pleasure of shopping there as for the need to buy things he couldn't store without a refrigerator.

As most city dwellers, Lucas abided by the anonymity shopping rules, "If I don't make eye contact, we'll pretend I'm invisible," retaining his privacy by not intruding on anyone else's space. Lucas did this as naturally as breathing. Therefore when the grocer greeted him, Lucas glanced at the man, nodded and looked away again. He passed a couple of women in the aisles who were shopping and ignored their frank appraisals. Using a hand-carried basket, he gathered the cans of food he had come after, added a bag of chips and one of cookies and a can of coffee.

When he approached the checkout counter, he noticed a lanky man wearing a sheriff's badge looking in his direction, but as he'd done with the others, he ignored the man's curious stare. The grocer rang up his purchases as Lucas waited patiently, his eyes memorizing the unique layout of the store in case he ever decided to use it in a book. When he was given the total, he reached in his pocket and paid in cash. Tucking his purchases under his arm, he left.

"See?" the grocer said to Sheriff Joe Odom. "He don't pass the time of day with nobody or even act friendly. Don't even meet your eyes when you look right at him."

"Yeah, I noticed that," the sheriff agreed.

"If you was to ask me, I think he seemed right edgy seeing you in here. Did you see how he kept looking up at the ceiling and toward the back of the store? I'm telling you, he's up to no good."

Joe nodded, his face grim. "I'll keep an eye on him, Fred. You can count on that." He tipped his hat as he left. "Give my regards to the missus."

FOR THREE DAYS Rainie managed to stay away from Lucas Dalton's cabin on the mountain. She needed time to think, to decide what she really wanted. Since her divorce, she had told anyone who would listen that she loved her newfound freedom and that marriage wasn't for her. But even before having met Lucas, her attitude had begun to change. She'd realized that she had married the wrong man the first time— a man with whom she had no common interest. Then Lucas Dalton had entered her life, and she and Lucas seemed to have much in common. She'd never expected to meet anyone like him.

But then she wasn't too sure what Lucas was offering. He had said their relationship wouldn't be a casual affair, but to her that meant love, and he had never mentioned love. And if he was suggesting a long, drawn-out dating relationship like Tom had with Eva Jean, she wasn't interested. She had heard too many derisive comments about how Tom and Eva Jean must be sleeping together after having dated all these years and must be afraid they would spoil their illicit affair by getting married. Rainie didn't want people gossiping about her personal business, and she wasn't interested in a love without permanent commitment. But hadn't she decided the week before that having Lucas as a lover was better than nothing at all? This was all too bewildering.

She tried to bury herself in work, but her daily tasks had become so routine they required little concentration, leaving her mind free to dwell on Lucas. He seemed to fill every corner of her consciousness.

Finally she gave up trying to avoid him and rode up to see him. The perverse side of her was prepared for possible rejection by him, and she was ready to turn her horse and gallop away, but he greeted her with a warm smile and nodded an acknowledgment of her presence. He was sitting on the top step of his porch, whittling on a piece of pink cedar. She stopped her horse a few yards from him. "If I'm invading your privacy, you just say the word, and I'll be gone," she stated without preamble.

Lucas quickly responded. "No. No, please stay. I'm glad you've come." Although his countenance held a welcome for her, his eyes looked troubled.

"I'm glad you want me to be here, but frankly I expected you to tell me to go away again."

"The last time you thought I said that, you cried."

"I did not," she quickly countered, then after consideration of his last statement, she asked, "Is that why you didn't ask me to leave just now? Behind your smile I can tell something is bothering you."

"I'm sorry," he said the smile finally reaching his eyes. "I've had a lot on my mind. I really am glad to see you." He motioned for her to sit next to him on the porch step, and she gratefully obliged. As he resumed his whittling, she studied his profile. There were a hundred questions she wanted to ask him, but he was such a private person, she was hesitant to ask them directly. Yet every time she saw him, her curiosity was intensified.

"What are you making?"

He paused for a minute. "Cedar shavings."

"I thought maybe it was going to be a bird or something."

"Nope, I'm not that creative. I like to whittle while I think. Sometimes it gives me a better focus."

"What were you thinking?"

"This and that." He glanced at her sideways and grinned, then he drew another long curl of pink wood from the stick. "I don't see how you figure this could ever look like a bird."

"I never thought that, exactly. I was just trying to be tactful about it. A lot of people support themselves by carving or weaving or other folk crafts." It had occurred to her that part of his hesitancy about getting involved with her might be because of the disparity in their earning capacities. If she could somehow broach the subject, she might be able to help him work through this issue. She waited to see if he would volunteer any information as to how he made a living. He didn't.

After a long pause, she said, "You know, I'm going to need more help when I increase my herd, and I like the way you handled Red the other day. Would you like a job?"

"No thanks."

"You don't have to give me your answer now. I pay a little more than minimum wage."

He smiled at her as if he were amused at the suggestion.

"Jobs are hard to find around here."

"I'm not looking for a job. Thanks for the offer, anyway."

Rainie was puzzled, but she didn't feel she should come right out and ask how he managed to support himself. It really wasn't any of her business, so she decided to drop it.

"The columbine is blooming down by the stream," she said to change the subject. "And the ground is thick with violets. Dogwood is blooming, too."

"Nothing is prettier than the mountains in springtime," he agreed. "I was walking by the water this morning and saw a thick carpet of moss with tiny white flowers growing in it, and the water rushing by was so clear I could see mossy pebbles on the creek bed. It's beautiful here."

"I love to hear you describe things," she said. "It's as if you paint pictures with your words."

He became silent and shoved his knife across the cedar stick, adding another shaving to the pile on the ground.

"Did that embarrass you? I didn't mean for it to. I was complimenting you."

"Thanks."

She sighed. No topic was automatically safe with him. Just when she was sure she had chosen an innocuous one, he would pull back like a turtle going into his shell.

"Lucas, I guess this really wasn't a good time for me to come. Maybe I should go."

Lucas reached out and touched her arm. "No, I want you to stay. I enjoy the time we spend together." She was sure his words were sincere.

"That sounds like you're encouraging me. Does that mean you've changed your mind about coming to visit me sometime? I've been wondering if I should ask you again."

"Is that an invitation or are you merely wondering?"

"It's an invitation. Supper. Tomorrow night."

"Yes, I would like that. Should I bring anything?"

Rainie couldn't believe his answer. Beaming him a radiant smile, she said, "Just come about seven. Can you find your way in the dark?"

"Unless the headlights in the Jeep have gone out, I'm sure I can."

"I didn't think your Jeep was running. But as narrow as the path is, I'm not sure even the Jeep would make it. It would be easier if you walk down, anyway. On foot, you just follow the narrow wagon road down the mountain. I had Oscar re-wire the gate so it's easier to open than it was before."

"Okay, I'll walk down."

"I'm easy to find. That old road passes behind my barns."

"I expect I could find you anywhere."

His words of endearment struck a chord in her heart, and she met his intense gaze. His eyes spoke volumes to her, but she was afraid to listen. She averted her eyes, and after swallowing the lump in her throat, she said, "Now that we've decided to share visits, why not let me loan you Red? He doesn't get nearly enough exercise. And you'd be doing me a favor by taking him," she added in sudden inspiration.

"A favor? In what way?"

"It would free up a stall for a mare I'm expecting to foal early," she improvised. "Right now she's in the feed lot with five other horses, but if you borrow Red, I can put her in the small lot that opens into the box stall. I'm afraid one of the other horses will kick her, and she's still in poor health."

"All right. I'll take Red for a while."

"I really appreciate it. Is your barn lot secure or should I send Billy up to repair it?"

"I can manage by myself, thanks. What kind of feed should I buy?"

"Oh, don't bother. I'll send up a sack. This time of year he doesn't need much. The grass is already high. You can ride him back up here tomorrow night after supper, if you'd like."

"All right."

"Well, I guess I should be getting back. I told Billy I'd work with Blaze again today. You're sure Red will be no trouble?"

"None at all."

They stood, and Rainie draped India's reins over her arm. "I'll walk you to the gate," he offered when she hesitated.

"Okay." Instead of mounting, she walked beside him and let the horse follow.

Lucas tossed away the stick he had been working on and folded his knife and put it in his pocket as they started down the road. "One of the things I was thinking about when you arrived was whether I could go see you. I've been concerned about you."

"About me?"

"I thought you must be upset."

"About what happened at your cabin the other night? No, not upset. Confused, maybe."

"I'm a bit confused myself." He bent and picked a tiny violet from beside a log covered in ferns. "Look. It's the same color as your eyes."

"Another beautiful compliment. For a hermit, you're pretty good at that. With a little practice, you could sweep a woman off her feet without half trying."

For a moment Lucas considered telling her the truth about his identity, but then it occurred to him that he might be wanting to reveal his secret simply to impress her. Rainie had said Jordan Lane was one of her favorite authors. Maybe he was subconsciously trying to sway her into falling in love with him by impressing her with his fame. And if she did fall in love with him, wouldn't that make it all the more painful when they eventually parted ways? Lucas was no scalp hunter, and he didn't want to trace his life with a trail of broken hearts. His thoughts were interrupted when Rainie grabbed his hand and drew him to a halt.

She stooped and pushed aside some glossy, heart-shaped leaves. "Look. Little brown jugs." The tiny brown flowers grew like a group of fairy jugs on the loamy ground. "I'm surprised to see any so early in the year."

"You love the woods, don't you? I can't imagine you in a city."

"I tend to bloom where I'm planted, as the saying goes. I prefer the woods and I love these mountains, but I also enjoyed the convenience of city life. It's just that I prefer who and where I am now. You aren't missing anything by not living in a city," she added to comfort him. "It's not all you think it would be." She hesitated and said, "Have you ever been in a city? A real one, I mean, not the county seat."

He smiled. "Yes."

"Of course, you have," she said hastily. "I didn't mean I thought you had never been out of the mountains." She wondered which city it had been and how long ago, but didn't want to embarrass him by asking. The mystery surrounding Lucas was almost impenetrable.

Lucas waited for her to ask the obvious question, but she didn't. One of the traits he found most intriguing about her was that she rarely did anything that he expected.

At the gate, he lifted the wire bale over the post and let her through. He was tempted to walk her the rest of the way and escape the empty afternoon, but dared not. He already felt terribly guilty that he wasn't writing, and knew it would be worse if he didn't even try to work.

"My house is just beyond those trees," she said. "The road passes through the apple orchard and from there the house is obvious. If you ever come and I'm not there, try the barn. By the way, don't let my dogs alarm you. They don't bite."

"I'll keep that in mind." As he started to fasten the gate between them, Rainie reached out and took his hand and Lucas responded by gently pulling her into his embrace and tenderly kissing her. Mutually, they parted, both reluctant to go. "Until tomorrow night, then," he offered.

"At seven. Earlier if you choose. You can help me cook. Or you can show up on time and be treated like company. Either way, I never stand on formalities."

"Somehow I didn't think you would."

"You do have a flashlight, don't you? It will come in handy."

"I have one."

Rainie turned away to get her horse and as Lucas fastened the gate, he let his eyes linger on the tantalizing curves of her jean's-clad derriere. With a shake of his head, he headed back up the mountain.

"Lucas?" she called after him.

He turned and looked back at her.

"You aren't a moonshiner are you?"

He laughed. "No."

"Okay." With a grin, she mounted her horse and rode away.

He watched her ride out of sight. She was fascinating and bewitching and maddening, all in equal doses. Obviously she was wondering how he managed to live with no visible means of support, but she was trying in her way not to be too intrusive. He wondered how many other guesses she would make.

One thing was for sure, she would never stumble upon his real occupation.

As he made his way back up the road, it occurred to him that one benefit in their blossoming relationship was that when he was with her, he didn't worry about not being able to write. Until her arrival that afternoon, he'd worried all day that he hadn't so much as opened the door to his office, but the worrying was pointless. And so was the time he spent staring at his nonproductive typewriter.

When he reached his cabin, he went to the barn lot and surveyed the fence. It looked in worse shape than it really was. The boards were rough and silvered from the weather, but in the area close to the barn, the fence was still sturdy. The gate latched with a rusty chain looped over a bent nail, but it was secure enough to pen a lazy horse like Red.

However, his inspection of the lower end of the lot, where the stream ran through, revealed some repair was needed. Lucas was whistling as he went after a hammer and nails and lumber from the barn.

The physical labor felt good after all the days of inactivity, so after he finished his repairs to the fence, he made a new feed box, as well. Then he added a few new slats to the hayrick, even though he didn't have a handful of straw to put in it.

Needing a rest, Lucas sat on the log threshold of the barn door that opened into the lot and leaned back against the doorframe. The log beneath him, which was part of the barn's foundation beam, was worn and cupped where countless horse and mule hooves had clipped it as they went in and out. He wiped the sweat from his brow with his handkerchief and mulled over the additional work that caring for Rainie's horse would entail. It had probably been a mistake to agree to take the animal, but it would mean he was certain to continue to see Rainie. Not that he wouldn't pursue her, if she suddenly decided not to come and see him. At this point he wasn't sure he could stop seeing her and still sleep nights. Besides, his taking the horse was doing her a favor.

As he blankly stared across the barn lot, he reflected on all the women he had known—millionaires and countesses and the would-be-famous, who thought their association with a well-known author would give them a boost up the ladder. Most of the women he had liked—Lucas tended to be interested in most people. A few he had liked a lot. One he had thought he loved, so he had married her, but soon found she was far more interested in his money and what it could buy than in him.

Christine was already remarried, to a man old enough to be her grandfather, but who had a new yacht and connections in Hollywood. Lucas felt he was well rid of her. She had always insisted on calling him Jordan. With a wry smile and twenty-twenty hindsight, he realized that should have given him a clue.

No woman could possibly be less like Christine than was Rainie. He had always been able to predict what his ex-wife would do in any situation. Rainie left him guessing on even the basics. Where Christine had been socially correct in every instance, Rainie was lax to the point of not caring if he showed up at the appointed time or if he came early and helped her cook dinner. Lucas loved that. As a creative person he wasn't all that fond of schedules and rules, and he tended to break them whenever they became at all restrictive. Only his book deadlines were sacrosanct. Here was a woman who would help him scatter the rest of life's regulations to the winds.

Lucas got up and walked down to the stream. Was he fooling himself? Could they ever work out a future? Maybe it was simply the springtime lure and romance of the mountains that made her seem so perfect for him. Surely at this stage of his life, he was beyond the summer-love syndrome. But would she fit into his life? Could he fit into hers?

Lucas wished like hell he hadn't chosen this time and place to fall in love.

RAINIE WAS STILL THINKING of Lucas as she rode into the orchard. Overhead were clouds of fluffy white apple blossoms tinged with the palest of pink. Industrious honeybees buzzed and hummed amid the flowering branches, and a carpet of tender green grasses surrounded the gnarled trunks. Spring always made her think of love. Was that what this was all about?

She let India settle into his quick walk as they neared the barn, and she had to duck to avoid the nearest limb. Surely she was old enough not to confuse hormones with love. Was two years of abstinence finally catching up with her?

The idea of making love with Lucas had obsessed her since the physical intimacy they'd shared the night she went to his cabin for supper. Rainie was no prude, but neither was she one to condone tumbling into bed with a man just because she desired him—certainly not in these days. She sensed that Lucas wasn't the sort to be morally lax, either, and perhaps he felt as much of a sense of commitment to her as she did to him.

He had been married before. She tried to picture a woman in that cabin, an apron tied around her waist and with curtains at the window, but she gave up. The cabin had Lucas's stamp all over it, and she couldn't imagine him living there with anyone else.

She rode into the barn and took care of India's needs, more from habit than conscious thought, as her mind was filled with Lucas Dalton. Blaze, in the stall next to India's, balefully eyed her, but nevertheless she went back out to the orchard. Blaze and his training could wait a few minutes longer. This was important.

She looked down at the bare ring finger on her left hand. She did want a permanent commitment and was no longer sure she could be satisfied with a mere affair.

In a few days Marla and Bob would be married. Maybe this was the reason she felt so lonely these days. She and Marla were close friends, and Rainie had been caught up in all the wedding plans.

She looked up at the tree-covered mountain slope where Lucas lived. Had there been no trees, she would have been looking right at his cabin. Was he up there thinking about her? Maybe he had gone back to his aimless whittling, and she wasn't on his mind at all. Rainie wondered darkly if this were a swing of the pendulum for her having been so resentful of Harry's workaholism. Lucas apparently didn't work at all.

She had always said that she only needed enough money to live in minimal comfort and to pay her bills. Now she was falling in love with a man who actually lived that philosophy. *Be careful what you wish for*, her mind taunted, *or you might get it*. She had never thought she would be tempted to spend the rest of her life with a jobless hermit.

The rest of her life? Rainie sighed. That phrase sounded like a life sentence in connection with Harry and like a promise of perennial paradise with Lucas.

But maybe he didn't want that at all. Rainie couldn't figure him out. He was such a mass of contradictions. Could anyone be as well self-educated as he appeared to be? As self-sufficient? She had a feeling she could spend years unraveling such a complex personality and still not fully understand him. He hadn't known where to look for the little brown jugs, but once when she had mentioned a Welsh pageant she had seen in nearby Millsburg, he had told her why the symbol for the Prince of Wales was a plume and that this was the reason that Princess Di's hat had been adorned with a feather for her wedding. How had he known all that? And how on earth did he hear that some uninformed news media person had said the feather looked silly? He would almost have had to watch the television coverage of the event to know that.

She walked to a nearby tree and looped her arm over the knotted lower branch. The golden bees hummed over her head, but she paid them no attention. Now that Lucas had come into her life and she'd fallen in love with him, she wasn't so sure she would ever be able to get him out again—even if she wanted to.

"I love him," she whispered to the apple tree. "I didn't plan to fall in love with him, but I have." She was reminded of one of her great-aunts who had once cautioned her never to date a man she wouldn't want to marry. She wondered what her aunt would say about this turn of events. And she wondered why the prospect of marrying a jobless hermit seemed so desirable.

7

RAINIE SPENT the day scrubbing and dusting and polishing her already clean and tidy house. Billy and Oscar didn't know what to make of this sudden burst of domesticity, and they teased her about having the governor out for supper. Rainie refused to rise to the bait, and made a great show of washing the dogs, instead.

As the afternoon waned, she started thinking about Lucas having to find his way to her house in the dark. She was one of those people who never get lost, but she wasn't so sure about him. He always seemed to stay close to his cabin.

She rummaged through a box of gift-wrap items and selected a large roll of bright yellow ribbon. Armed with the ribbon and scissors, Rainie went up the path, tying neat bows on trees to mark the way. Now he couldn't possibly get lost.

However, as she went back to her house, she recalled a song from several years back about tying yellow ribbons on an old oak tree. In the song, the ribbons were a symbol of love. Would he think she was saying she loved him? And was that the subconscious reason she had picked the yellow over the red or blue ones? She groaned, hoping he had never heard of the song. Living as he did, that was possible. And what if he took offense that she had marked what admittedly was a fairly well-defined old road, as though he might be too inept to find his way? But she couldn't concern herself with that, for she had too much else to do.

Dinner presented another problem. She didn't want to cook anything pretentious like filet of beef béarnaise, or something that could turn out a disaster like a soufflé, yet a pot of chili was too simple. Was he a steak and potato man or was he vegetarian? Recalling he had served her canned stew, she ruled out the latter.

After great deliberation and time spent pouring over a half dozen cookbooks she had received as wedding presents, Rainie threw her hands up and decided to go with what she cooked best—Mexican food. Thanks to "care packages" from her mother, Rainie kept her pantry stocked with brands of tortillas and hot sauces that the grocery in Lupine didn't carry. A quick inventory verified that she still had enough avocados and tomatoes, so she rolled up her sleeves and went to work.

By seven o'clock her kitchen was filled with the tantalizing aromas of carne asada, arroz, frijoles and enchiladas. Guacamole was in the refrigerator; flan was cooling beside it. But her kitchen looked like a disaster.

Moving at top speed, Rainie shoved the pots and pans and cooking utensils into the dishwasher, then frantically wiped the countertop clean. She had already changed into the skirt she had chosen for the evening, but the blouse she was wearing was an old one. She had left all her aprons behind in Louisville as a gesture of her independence, an impulsive act she sometimes regretted, and knew from experience that she shouldn't risk soiling one of her favorite blouses while cooking.

She was still scrubbing the kitchen cabinet doors when she heard a knock on her back door. He was here! As usual her dogs hadn't bothered to bark. She ran a nervous hand over her hair and licked her lips to see if she was wearing lipstick. If only she had been more organized! She caught a glimpse of her reflection in the kitchen window and groaned. She was still wearing the work shirt! Without a pause, she ripped it off and threw it, along with the soiled cup towels, into the cabinet under the sink.

Grabbing her fresh blouse from the back of a kitchen chair and buttoning it as fast as she could, she made her way to the door. As she stuffed in her shirttail and smoothed her skirt, it dawned on her that Lucas might not like Mexican food. Some people didn't. She ate it so often she considered it normal fare, but would someone who had always lived in Tennessee? Maybe Lucas hated it! Marla had once said it was an acquired taste.

She flung open the door with such speed Lucas took a step back. "Come in," she said breathlessly. "If you hate Mexican food, I can cook something else."

He stepped inside and looked around appreciatively. He was in an open dinette area that was separated from the kitchen by a butcher-block counter. The rooms were white with accents of leaf green and peach. The countertops and table and chairs were natural wood. He hoped Rainie hadn't noticed that he was intentionally avoiding looking at her. He needed a moment for his pulse to return to normal. When he had knocked on the door, he had naturally been facing the glass upper section and had been amazed to see Rainie yank off her blouse, throw it under the sink, and put on another one. The totally unexpected vision of her rounded breasts cupped in her sheer lace bra had sent a blaze of desire through him that had left him shaken. He still wasn't too sure he could speak.

"You do, don't you?" She hurried back into the kitchen. "It's no trouble at all. I can fix . . . soup. Chicken soup. And crackers. I know you like crackers."

"Rainie!" He caught her as she grabbed a can of soup from the pantry. "Rainie, slow down. I like Mexican food."

"You're just saying that so I won't be embarrassed that I didn't ask you earlier."

"No, I'm not."

"I don't believe you."

"I *love* it."

She narrowed her eyes and put her head to one side to study him. "Are you sure?"

"I grew up on chili and tamales and enchiladas."

Rainie wasn't sure she believed him, but he looked sincere. "Okay. We'll have Mexican food." She put several flour tortillas into an earthenware dish, and as she was reaching for the lid she saw her reflection in the glass of the window over the sink. She stopped and looked at her image again. If she could see herself in the lighted kitchen, and if Lucas had been outside in the darker yard . . . She looked over at the door, which also had no window curtain, and a deep blush began to rise on her cheeks.

"Do you want those tortillas warmed?" Lucas was asking.

"Yes," she managed to stammer. "Warmed." She handed the covered dish to him without making eye contact.

He went to her microwave and pressed the button that opened the door. As casually as if he did this every day, he punched in the correct amount of time and started the machine.

Rainie stared at him. How did Lucas, who lived without electricity, know how to operate a microwave? She forgot her embarrassment in her surprise.

"Do we eat in here?" he asked.

Rainie remembered where she was and what she was doing. "I forgot to set the table!" She went to a wall of drawers and cabinets and took out a serape-design tablecloth she had bought on her last visit to San Antonio.

"Where are the plates?"

"There. In the second cabinet."

She spread the cloth over the wooden table and evened the edges. Lucas put two fiesta red plates on the cloth and looked at her for further instruction. "Silverware is in the top drawer on the right of the sink." Rainie frowned at the cabinet beneath the sink. *Had he been looking in the window and could he have seen her from that angle?* She stepped back nearer the door and tried to recall exactly where she had been standing.

"Are these the ones you want to use?" he asked, holding up a fork.

Rainie jerked around to look at him. "Yes. Yes, I use the good ones these days. There's no sense in not getting any use out of them. If silver plate is used regularly, it doesn't have to be polished." Her eyes widened. "The enchiladas!"

She hurried to the oven and pulled out a sizzling pan of food, which she liberally topped with grated Monterey Jack. Anticipating her need, Lucas put a trivet on the table, and she placed the dish of enchiladas on it. As she ladled up the rice, beans, and carne asada into the serving dishes, she told Lucas where the wineglasses were kept and asked him to pour the wine.

To make the table setting more intimate, she put two fat, cream-colored candles on each end and lit them. "I made flan for dessert," she said as she took the guacamole from the refrigerator, praying that luck was with her and the avocados hadn't turned dark. Fortunately the guacamole was exactly the right shade of green.

"You went to a lot of trouble," he said. "I only fed you canned stew."

"But it was very *good* canned stew. This was no trouble really. It's nice to have someone to cook for." To her surprise she found she meant it. She had never expected to enjoy cooking again.

"It gets old eating alone," he agreed, "and this looks great."

They sat down opposite one another, and Rainie served his plate with a generous portion of enchiladas. "Careful. It's hot."

"Good. The night's turned chilly. Coming through the woods felt ten degrees colder than in the clearing."

"I guess the stream cools it off."

"I'll be glad for all these jalapeños on the return trip."

"I'm not much on gardening, but my mother sends me home with pepper plants every spring. I raise enough to last me through the winter. Lupine can provide the basic American staples, but I have to write my parents to send tortillas and so forth."

He nodded. "Roan Oak is even more limited. It's got a great little store, though—things hanging from the ceiling and there are bags of cow feed in one corner. It oozes charm and character, but I have to drive to the county seat if I want anything special."

Rainie thought there was something peculiar about his observation. "It's odd you would see it that way since you grew up here. I wasn't able to appreciate the charm and uniqueness of San Antonio until I had lived away from it."

"Frijoles?" Lucas asked as he passed her the beans.

"I should have encouraged you to come earlier," she said. "I'd like for you to meet Billy and Oscar. They're almost like family. Or maybe you already know them. The Franks and Williams families have been here for generations."

"Nope, can't say that I do. Say, this is great! If you go out of the horse business you could always open a restaurant."

"In Lupine? I've finally been accepted, but if I were to go into competition with the café, I might become an outcast."

"You're right. People do tend to stick together around here."

A small frown creased Rainie's brow. Lucas had such an odd way of putting things, almost as if he didn't consider himself to be a local.

After supper Rainie added their dirty dishes to the dishwasher and turned it on while Lucas switched channels on the small TV on the kitchen countertop. She was gratified to see his obvious enjoyment at getting to see television, but she was also baffled by his apparent familiarity with the current season's programs. Lucas was definitely a man of mystery.

"Come out to the barn," she said as the dishwasher began its cycle. "I have something I want to show you."

As Lucas had said, the night was cool, and Rainie walked quickly across the lawn, illuminated only by a half moon that hung low in the night sky like a silver ornament. Stars spangled the expanse of blackness overhead, and a breeze from the mountain slopes brought the scent of evergreens.

When Rainie turned on the lights in the barn, the horses in the stalls pricked their ears in interest.

Rainie stopped in front of Red's stall and affectionately patted his rump while he munched on a mouthful of hay. "When you get ready to leave, I'll show you which saddle is his," she said. "I'm assuming you want to ride him back to your place. The trip up will be much faster and easier on horseback." He nodded his agreement.

In the far stall, one that was considerably larger than most of the others, was penned a thin-necked, dark brown horse. Lucas had never seen one look so bad. "This is one of your animals?"

"She is now. This is one of the horses I saved from a monster who lives down the road."

"She looks terrible!"

"He was starving them. This one is pregnant, so I took her away from the others."

"I remember you mentioning a mare that was about to foal. You said you needed me to take Red so you'd have stall space for her." He looked around. "It looks to me as if you have plenty of room."

Rainie ignored his observation. "I'm worried about her. Bob Pollard says she won't foal until early next month, but I think he's wrong. What do you think?"

Lucas studied the animal. "I don't know much about horses, but she looks overdue to me."

"Maybe it's because her neck and hips are so skinny," Rainie said hopefully. "I sure hope I'm wrong. Bob and Marla are getting married tomorrow and will be on their honeymoon all next week. I think this mare will need all the help she can get when the time comes."

"If he's a vet, he must be able to judge these things."

"Normally, yes. But he has wedding nerves to the point where I'm surprised he can remember his own name."

Lucas opened the stall and went in to take a closer look. The mare snuffled and moved her lips over the palm of his hand as he stroked her nose. "I like the smell of a clean barn," he said. "It strikes some chord in me."

"I'm surprised she'll let you touch her. Normally she's scared to death of men, even of Billy."

"Animals like me." He ran his hand over the horse's rough coat and patted her companionably. "The laws aren't strict enough against animal abuse."

"I agree."

After rubbing the mare behind the ears, Lucas came back out to join Rainie. "I hope she makes it."

"As bad as this one looks, there's another one that's worse. Bob wants to put her down, but I can't give up yet. She's old, and her age is working against her."

They left the barn and Lucas helped Rainie close the heavy door to keep in the animals' warmth. As they crossed the yard he nodded toward two of the dogs. "You don't have great watchdogs."

"I know. They watch everything that goes on, but they don't bother to bark. You'd think at least one of them would care if a stranger is on the place." She shook her head in resignation. "The sheriff is a friend of mine, and he even gave me a German shepherd puppy once. But instead of him teaching the others to bark at strangers, it happened the other way around."

"Would they protect you if you were threatened?"

"Let's just say if I ever have a burglar, I hope he steals the dog food first. They all feel strongly about being fed."

Lucas laughed. "You aren't afraid, then?"

"No. Not really." She hoped he wouldn't ask about loneliness. And he didn't.

They went inside and Lucas washed his hands at the kitchen sink. Before she thought to get a towel for him, he opened the door beneath the sink and dried his hands on the one she had tossed there as she changed her blouse. Rainie felt the painful blush return.

As Lucas followed her into the living room, he seemed not to notice her embarrassment, though she was sure he was not only aware of her bright red cheeks, but understood the reason for her discomfort. She was afraid he might say something about it.

In the center of the room he turned and looked right at her, but she averted her eyes. "I like your house," he commented.

Grateful for normal conversation, she quickly responded, "I call this style Granny Provincial. Lots of quilts and laces and crafts."

"It feels comfortable."

She smiled with relief. "That's what first drew me to this place. It felt like home the minute I stepped in the door. I fell in love with it at first sight. Do you believe in that sort of thing?"

"Love at first sight? Not until recently."

She faltered. His tone suggested he was referring to people, not places. "I meant in a house having its own character, almost a personality."

For a moment he watched her in silence, then picked up a magazine from the coffee table. "Sure I do. I've seen houses that feel uncomfortable or angry or happy. I guess everyone has experienced that."

"I guess. I never thought you had been around that much."

"I'm not a chipmunk, Rainie. I do see people and go into houses."

"Oh. Of course, you do. At first I thought you didn't have the usual conveniences in your cabin, like electricity, because you were Amish or something. I mean, you do have a beard and all."

He laughed as if that amused him a great deal. "No, I'm not Amish. Not by a long shot. My cabin's inconveniences are purely geographical."

"Now see? There you go talking like that again! I can't believe you've picked up all these conversational skills purely from reading books."

He didn't answer.

"You constantly amaze me," she said as she sat on the sofa. "You seem to be such a contradiction."

He flipped through the pages of the magazine as if he were trying to decide how to answer her, then put it down and came to sit beside her. "Does it bother you that I don't seem to be what you think I should be? Would you like it better if I were, say, from Memphis?"

"No," she said with a quick laugh. His eyes were velvety dark, and she could smell the faint aroma of his cologne. "No, of course not. I like you just the way you are."

"You do?" He rested his arm along the back of the couch and almost absentmindedly fingered her hair. Rainie felt the caress as if he were touching her bare skin.

"I've had my fill of city men. No, you being from any-where but the mountain would be a definite turnoff for me."

"It would?"

She tried unsuccessfully to read his eyes. All she could see, however, was the intensity of his expression. He looked as if he were memorizing her features and asking that she meet him in some unspoken agreement. His fingers became bolder and rubbed the skin at her nape. Excitement sparked the pulse in Rainie's throat.

"Maybe you'd like me better," he continued in his deep, sensuous voice, "if I had seen more of the world and had made an impression on it."

She tried to smile, but her lips felt swollen, as if he were al-ready kissing them. "How many people can do that? You'd have to be awfully rich or famous for the world to know you exist." He ran his thumb over the line of her jaw and brushed the curve of her lower lips. Rainie had trouble remembering to breathe. "I like you exactly the way you are," she whis-pered, afraid of breaking the spell that he was weaving be-tween them.

"Yes," he agreed softly. "This is much better. You care for me and not for what I've accomplished."

"It doesn't matter to me that you haven't changed the world, Lucas. I'm only interested in you."

He leaned closer until his lips were a breath away from her own. "You do mean that, don't you, Rainie? You do care for me?"

Her eyes mirrored the love in her heart as she replied. "Can't you tell? I didn't know I could still feel as much for anyone as I do for you."

Gently he kissed her as if she were so infinitely precious that a sudden move might dissolve her into mist. He drew back a bit and gazed deep into her eyes. Rainie knew what he was silently asking, but she couldn't speak the words. Not until she heard them from his lips.

"I want you," he said in a voice so quiet she heard him mainly with her heart. "Lord help me, but I love you."

She wondered at his phrasing, but only for an instant. "You love me?" Her eyes widened with incredulous hope. "Me?"

"Yes. I know it's too soon and that it's all wrong, but it's true. I love you."

Her deep blue eyes sparkled with dewy tears as she replied, "I love you, Lucas. I've tried hard not to love you, but it's true."

He leaned his forehead forward to touch hers. "What are we going to do about this?"

She smiled and rubbed her cheek against the softness of his beard. "I guess we'll do what people have always done."

"I'm not asking you to marry me." His voice sounded forced, as if the words were hard for him to say. "I can't."

"I'm not sure I would say yes." She saw the surprise in his eyes. "It's not that I don't want you. Right now I feel as if this will last forever and ever. But I've thought that before, and I was wrong. I don't want to rush into anything."

He cupped her face in his hands, looking as if there were something he felt he had to say. Rainie put her fingers gently on his lips. "No, Lucas. Don't feel you have to do or say anything. You and I aren't children, and we don't need promises that may or may not prove to last. I love you and you love me. That's enough."

"Is it? Is it really that simple?"

"Between us it is."

He kissed her and she tasted his warm breath and clean skin. When his strong arms tightened around her, she responded by holding him closer and kissing him with growing passion.

"Rainie! What are you doing to me?" he ground out when he lifted his lips from hers. "When you kiss me like that I can feel you giving yourself to me."

"That's exactly what I was doing."

"No ties," he murmured. "No commitments."

"I want you," she sighed.

A muscle tightened in Lucas's jaw and she wondered if he was about to leave her. A war was being waged in his eyes, making them nearly black and so piercing she could almost see his thoughts. Then, apparently having made whatever decision he was wrestling with, he stood and held out his hand to her.

For a second she hesitated, still not sure of whether he intended to stay or to leave. Then she placed her small hand in his, and he drew her to her feet. Almost roughly he pulled her to him and kissed her, and she wondered if he were regretting his decision. Then he bent and scooped her up as if she weighed no more than a child.

Rainie smiled and pressed her face against the pulse that raced in his throat, because she knew now what his decision had been.

Somehow, Lucas carried her unerringly to her bedroom. When he reached her bed, he hesitated and looked deep into her eyes, giving her one last chance to change her mind. His face was as fiercely proud as a barbarian warrior's, and Rainie felt a delicious shiver run through her. "I want you," she repeated.

He laid her on the bed and reached down to pull off her shoes. As if he were treasuring the moment, he slowly ran his hand up the silken length of her leg, beneath her skirt, and cupped her buttocks. "Rainie, there's something I ought to tell you. I'm—"

Again she put her fingers to his lips to silence him. "Don't tell me any 'oughts' or 'shoulds.' I know all I need to know about you. I know you've known other women and that you must have cared for them, but you love me. That means they don't count. You don't ever have to tell me anything unless you want to."

"Are you an angel? Can any human be as open and giving as you are?"

"That's love." She drew his face down and kissed him with all the desire that she held for him.

Lucas eased his hand over her hips, his thumb hooked into the top of her panty hose. Rainie shifted to assist him, and he swept them off her legs, one stocking at a time.

As he began to unbutton her blouse she had to ask, "How long were you looking in the window of my back door before I opened it?"

He grinned and mischief danced in his eyes. "Long enough."

"That's what I thought."

"I'll buy you some curtains for your birthday," he teased as he leisurely opened the front of her blouse. Desire darkened his eyes as he exposed the lacy cups of her bra. "I don't want to share this view with anyone."

She let him pull the blouse away, and he half lifted her to release the fastener of her bra. Rainie felt her cheeks pinken. She had always thought her breasts were too small—a sentiment Harry had reinforced on several occasions. But when Lucas tossed the bra aside, the reverent expression on his face dispelled her fears.

"Beautiful," he murmured. "You're so beautiful." He lowered his lips to her breast, kissing first one pouting nipple, then the other.

As his mouth closed over the coral bud, Rainie gasped with pleasure. His tongue flicked her nipple to throbbing eagerness, as he drew it deeper into his mouth, Rainie felt the accompanying desire all the way into the pit of her stomach.

Her body responded with a surge of passion, and she arched her back to increase the pressure of his mouth on her breast.

After Lucas unfastened her skirt and slipped it and her panties off in one fluid motion, he lingered for a long moment over her, feasting his eyes on her body while his hands explored her willing flesh. Her breath quickened at his tender touch, and she gloried in the desire she saw in his face, because she knew it was the sight and feel of her that had put it there. She had never before seen herself in the role of temptress, but she could see it now.

Slowly she sat up and her hair fell over her slender shoulder. Noses and lips almost touching, she gazed deep into his eyes as she began to unbutton his shirt. He met her gaze as if he would touch her soul with his, and he covered both her breasts with his palms as she unfastened his shirt.

Rainie pulled away the garment and lowered her eyes to his torso. He was lean and tanned, and muscles ridged in his belly and curved over his taut chest. She ran her hands over the warm skin of his powerful arms and relished the feel of his firm flesh. "You're beautiful, too," she said. "And sexy as all get out."

He laughed as he reached behind her to pull down the covers. His chest grazed her nipples, and Rainie felt another rush of excitement.

Lucas stood and finished removing his clothes as she rolled onto the fresh sheet. Her hair spread about her head like a skein of silk, and she made no effort to hide her body beneath the covers. Lucas watched as her eyes traveled over the rest of his body, and his expression showed her he was gratified to see her seductive smile.

"Beautiful," she repeated.

He lay beside her, matching his large body to her smaller one. She nestled in his arms, her breasts mounding against his chest, her hips touching his hips. "It's as if we were made to fit together," he said. "You're so small, I was afraid . . ."

She shook her head. "Isn't it wonderful how these things work out? I'd say you're just about perfect."

As he lovingly caressed her, she responded to his touch. Rainie was made for loving, and she had no compunction about pleasing him or about being pleased. As they explored each other's body, Lucas felt his love for her fill him to over-flowing. He loved her more than he wanted her, and he wanted her so badly he ached.

He drew out their pleasure, learning how to kiss and lick and touch her so that she bloomed for him. Rainie held nothing back. She was as honest in her loving as she was in everything else. She titillated his body with her fingers, she kissed him, and she ran her pink tongue over his skin until he thought he would burst from his desire for her. As she learned what gave him pleasure, he found his passion for her becoming a need.

Clearly his need was answered by her own, for Rainie took the initiative and angled her hips so that he entered her as easily as breathing. Lucas fought for control. He wanted to ravish her—to plunge deep into her and lose himself in completion—but he held himself in check.

Sensuously he moved, finding her rhythm and matching it. Again his love overcame his passion and as he pushed deep into her hot body, he was rewarded by the pulsing sensation that meant she was reaching her peak.

Rainie cried out and held on to him as if she would never let him go. Lucas cradled her in his embrace and marveled that he could love her so much. He loved her more than he loved himself!

Again he began to move, drawing her back into quick-ened response, as if she could never have enough of him. This time when she reached her pinnacle, Lucas was unable to hold back. He pressed deep into her silken warmth and felt his universe explode. Together they rode the hot waves of consummated passion. He felt his soul touch hers and intertwine with hers, and never quite leave.

"I love you," he said as they lay facing each other, sharing the same pillow. "I love you as I've never loved anyone." He couldn't keep the marvel from his voice. This was a miracle that was too precious to savor alone. "I love you."

"I know," she said, her voice soft with satisfaction. "Nothing like this has ever happened to me, either. Not like this."

"What will become of us?" he asked huskily, thinking of all the important facts about himself that she never even suspected.

She smiled, not realizing he meant the question as anything but a rhetorical one. "We'll love each other, and we'll wait and see. Just like all lovers do."

Lucas held her and stroked her soft hair and wished his life were really as simple as Rainie had been led to believe.

8

LUCAS AWOKE SLOWLY, trying to hang on to the dream as he gradually became fully conscious. The dream stayed with him. He saw a band of settlers building a cabin and hacking a free life out of the wilderness. Then the dream skipped time as dreams tend to do, and he saw the pioneers a few years later with a young family. The woman, who bore a strong resemblance to Rainie, was toil-worn, but when she looked at her husband—Lucas had cast himself in that role—she seemed to glow.

His eyes flew open. That was the missing link! The puzzle piece he had been sweating over for weeks! He had started his novel in the wrong time frame!

All at once the story unfolded in his mind. It should start with the parents, which would explain why the heroine and hero were the way they were. Two families! His thoughts tumbled feverishly. Two families whose roots and futures were inextricably linked!

He rolled over and swung his legs out of bed. In front of him was a wall papered in rows of delicate flowers. The window curtain was sheer, white lace. This wasn't his cabin.

Startled, Lucas turned and looked at the other side of the bed. Rainie lay there curled in a deep sleep, her dark hair fanned over the white pillowcase. A feeling of tenderness stole over him as he watched her sleep. They had spent most of the night making love, and he knew she was tired. The faint light through the curtain told him dawn was just breaking.

He drew the down comforter up around her bare shoulders and kissed her on the cheek. Rainie smiled in her sleep and sighed with contentment.

Lucas got out of bed and gathered his clothing into a bundle. Tiptoeing, he left the room and closed the bedroom door behind him. Hastily, he dressed in the cool hall. He didn't want to wake Rainie. She needed her rest, and he was afraid if he didn't get to his typewriter quickly, he might lose the illusive thought that would end his writer's block.

He let himself out of the house and stretched. All his muscles felt pleasantly stiff. For a minute he considered going back in and waking Rainie just to tell her again that he loved her, but he decided against it. He could think of no reasonable explanation, short of the truth, for his urgent need to get back to his cabin and his typewriter. And he was too concerned, at this point, about the vulnerability of this new relationship to risk admitting he'd deceived her.

He found the tack room in the barn with no trouble, and as Rainie had indicated, each animal's tack was clearly labeled. He wanted to be gone before Rainie's hired help arrived, in order to save her any embarrassment his presence at dawn might cause. Within minutes he had saddled Red and was galloping through the dew-frosted orchard.

How obvious it all seemed now that he thought of starting the book a generation earlier! Even as he wondered he had missed it for so long, he knew the answer—he had spent more time concentrating on his writer's block than on spinning a dream. He had read and re-read the outline until the words no longer inspired any visions, and Lucas had never been able to write until the story unfolded in living color in his mind. Rainie had changed all that. She had given him something else to occupy his mind. If he hadn't already loved her, he would have fallen in love with her for that reason alone.

When he reached the cabin, he turned Red loose in the feed lot and hung the saddle from a rope in the tack room on the off chance there were leather-hungry rats lurking in the loft, then he ran to his cabin. Not bothering to bathe or shave or change clothes, Lucas yanked open the door to his tiny office. Ripping out the offensive, curled paper in his typewriter, he threw it away in defiance of his writer's block. Purposefully he seated himself at his desk, rolled a fresh sheet of paper into the machine, and began to type feverishly.

RAINIE WOKE UP with a smile on her lips and love warming her heart. Sleepily she reached out, expecting to find Lucas's warm body, but instead touched only cool sheets. Her eyes flew open. Lucas was gone.

She sat up and looked around as if he might be standing about somewhere. "Lucas?" she called out. There was no answer.

For a minute she had the eerie sensation that she might have dreamed about making love, but then she turned and saw the rumpled sheets on the other side of the bed. Her stiff muscles confirmed she had spent the night with Lucas. Rainie lay back and sensuously stretched, much as a cat would. She certainly had never had a dream that wonderful.

With a satisfied smile, she fetched her robe from the closet. Lucas must be in the bathroom, she decided. But when she went into the hall, she could see the bathroom door was open, and the room was obviously empty. "Lucas?" she called again.

Somewhat confused, she belted her robe and checked the living room and kitchen. Both were silent and empty. For a moment she was vaguely disoriented, but then from her kitchen window she saw Billy riding Blaze in the exercise arena and Oscar working under the hood of the farm truck, and her world was suddenly in focus again. She wheeled and stared at the clock. "Damn! Nine o'clock?"

With haste, she returned to her bedroom and dressed for the day.

Billy and Oscar greeted her with nonchalance, but she couldn't help wondering whether they had correctly deduced the reason she had slept late. They might even have seen Lucas leaving. It wasn't that she felt guilty, but with so little for people to do in Lupine, gossip was a primary form of entertainment, and she didn't want to be the subject. If Billy and Oscar did know that Lucas had spent the night, there was nothing she could do about it now. She was, however, thankful, that if they knew, they were gentlemen enough not to say anything about it to her.

Quickly she set about her daily chores, knowing that idly daydreaming of the night before would only fuel their curiosity. She tried to postpone her thoughts of Lucas until her work was finished, but it was impossible. It had been a long time since she'd made love, and every movement of her body seemed to trigger a physical sensation that reminded her of the night before.

Seeing that Red was gone rekindled her niggling concern that Lucas hadn't said goodbye. True, she had never spent the night with a lover before, and she wasn't sure how these things were done, but she had assumed Lucas would wait around for a cup of coffee, or at least tell her he was leaving. Surely he knew no one slept late on a working horse farm.

As she saddled January, she wondered what to make of Lucas. Did his not telling her goodbye mean he didn't really love her? Maybe he regretted having said he did. Or perhaps this was just a line he had used. She didn't know what to think. He had certainly acted as if he meant his words of love. She had been sure she had seen love in his eyes, but maybe that was because hers were so full of love.

She mounted the horse and rode him into the corral for his workout. January pranced in the cool air, but was too well-schooled to act up. She nudged him into a quick trot to warm him up.

She loved Lucas. Last night had driven away any lingering doubts. She loved him and was ready to match her life to his, when he said the word, but then she remembered him saying he wasn't asking her to marry him. A frown replaced her smile. If two people were single and in love, wasn't it only logical that they marry? If it was a matter of him wanting to live in his cabin instead of in her house, that was no problem. Rainie was willing to ride down the mountain to work with her animals. That would leave him alone all day to do whatever it was what he did to fill the hours. Certainly he knew she wasn't marrying him for his money. The idea brought back her smile. Lucas didn't have any money.

Or was she rushing matters? Rainie knew she had a bad habit of doing that. Marla had once said jumping to conclusions was Rainie's favorite sport. Maybe the love she felt for Lucas wouldn't last. She felt as if it would, for it seemed to be the forever-after kind, but didn't all love seem that way at first? If not, what could explain why so many people married, thinking it was permanent, then later decided they'd married the wrong person and had to go through divorce. She loved Lucas more than she had ever loved Harry, but was it a love that would endure all the ups and downs of life? Did anyone ever know?

She had January reverse direction and drop back to the flowing walk that made his black mane ripple over his arched neck. Billy waved to her as he rode Blaze back to the barn and she returned the gesture. That, too, was a reminder of Lucas—a reminder that she should have thought to be more discreet.

She worked the horse for an hour, trying to concentrate on his timing and gaits, but her mind kept drifting back to Lucas. She was glad when she saw the sheriff's car pull around to the barn and park.

With a wave, she rode to the fence and dismounted. She opened the gate and led the horse through. "Hi, Tom. I'll bet you've come after those tabby kittens. I'll find a box to keep them corralled until you can get to Eva Jean's house."

"Make it a tall one. I can't drive and juggle cats all at the same time."

Rainie handed January's reins to Billy and ducked into the storeroom. "How about this one?" she said as she emerged.

"Great." Tom walked with her to the steps that led to the hayloft. "I've been talking to Joe Odom about that stranger."

"Odom? The sheriff at Roan Oak? I assumed the stranger had gone on his way by now."

"Nope. He's still hanging around. Joe saw him buying groceries one day last week. Said the man is sure peculiar."

"That's not against the law." She stepped onto the plank floor where the hay was swept back from the stairwell. "Don't trip on that uneven board."

Tom stepped over the loose board onto the hay. "Being peculiar's not against the law, but kidnapping sure is. That Jordan Lane fellow is still missing."

"Still? I saw something on the news about it a week or so ago, but I thought he must have been found by now."

"Not a hair of him. His folks say they still haven't been contacted for ransom, either."

"Maybe he wasn't kidnapped at all. Maybe he has amnesia or something."

"Stuff like that doesn't happen in real life," Tom scoffed. "That's just in books and movies."

"No, it's not. It may not be common, but it happens. When my youngest brother was on the high school football team, he had amnesia for nearly an hour once. He'd been tackled and had hit his head on the goal post."

"The FBI thinks Lane was kidnapped."

"Maybe he was in a wreck and hasn't been found yet." She bent to pick up a fat yellow kitten from atop a bale of hay. "Wouldn't that be sad? I love Jordan Lane's books." She pointed to where three kittens were tumbling over each other in the loose hay. "There's the other one."

Tom scooped up the pale orange ball of fluff. "Whatever has happened to him, I'll bet that stranger has something to do with it. You be careful."

"I'm always careful, Tom." She smiled at the sight of the tiny kitten in the sheriff's large, rough hands. "These babies will keep Eva Jean amused."

"I sure hope so. She's still pining over losing that old tomcat. Between you and me, I never did see what she liked about him. He had a rotten disposition."

"Well, these don't." She laughed at the kitten who was trying to eat her fingers. "Tell her to feed them kitten chow while they're babies."

"I bought a big bag of it on my way out here. She's all set." He put the kitten in the cardboard box and said, "Are you going to the wedding this afternoon?"

"Marla will skin me if I don't. I'm her matron of honor."

"I figured you would be. It's good to see old Bob settling down. Marla's a fine woman."

"So is Eva Jean," Rainie teased. "I guess you two will be next."

Tom laughed. "Don't you go putting ideas in her head. She's hard enough to manage as it is."

Rainie grinned as she put the kitten she'd been holding in with the other one. "She should take them in for their shots as soon as Bob and Marla are back from their honeymoon."

"I'll tell her."

"And if they keep her awake at night, tell her to put a ticking clock near their bed. I've heard that calms them down."

"Don't worry. Eva Jean will take care of them."

Rainie nodded. The kittens were going to a good home, and she had never had any intention of keeping them all. She followed the sheriff back down the steps and outside.

He squinted up at the sky. "Looks like we're in for a storm."

Rainie lifted her head. The sky looked bruised and angry against the mountain, and dark clouds were reaching for the sun. "We could use some rain."

"That's the truth." Tom Hanford opened the back door of his car and put the box of kittens on the seat. "Well, I'd better be going. I want to surprise Eva Jean with them during her lunch break."

"Tell her if they don't work out she can bring them back."

"I will, but if I know Eva Jean, she'll fall in love with them on the spot." He opened the driver's door. "You remember what I said about being careful. If you see this stranger, you call me right away."

"Okay." She smiled indulgently. "I will." She knew she wouldn't recognize the stranger if she saw him, because she knew almost no one from Roan Oak. Besides, the idea of a kidnapper hanging out in Lupine was ludicrous. If she were a kidnapper, she would head for a city where no one would know or care if she were an outsider.

She went back into the barn where Billy was brushing January. "How did he do?" he asked.

"Fine. You know January. All he needs is somebody to sit on top of him. He knows all the ropes. How's Blaze coming along?"

"Okay, I guess. His mouth seems tough. I don't think he'll be the horse we hoped he'd be."

"I've noticed the same thing. Maybe it's a mistake to keep him. We don't want to breed in bad qualities just because an animal looks good."

Billy nodded. "Let's give him a bit longer. He's stubborn, and he may still be fighting the bridle."

"I agree. There's no rush."

He nodded toward the back of the barn. "The chestnut mare is acting funny."

"Funny in what way?" Rainie looked back at the brood stall.

"She's pacing and looking wild-eyed."

"Could be the storm. Lightning bothers some animals more than others."

"Maybe, but she didn't act that way last week in that little rain we had."

Rainie mentally added Billy's observation to the list of things she needed to check on that day. For the next few hours she worked extrahard to make up for having slept in that morning and the time she would miss because of the wedding that afternoon. Despite her activity, however, Lucas was never far from her mind.

At two o'clock she had to stop what she was doing and get ready for the wedding. She found Oscar and said, "I have to hurry so I won't be late. Billy said the mare is acting nervous. Will you check her before you leave?"

The man nodded. "I reckon it's the weather. I feel edgy, too."

Rainie jogged to the house and showered, then carefully applied her makeup. She seldom wore makeup, so this task took longer than she had expected. Hastily she shimmied into the cornflower-blue bridesmaid dress and wriggled around, working the zipper up the back. As she rarely wore dresses, the chiffon skirt felt strange against her legs. She slid her stockinged feet into high-heeled sandals and grabbed up her

Sunday purse. Time was ticking away, and she knew Marla must be wondering where she was. Rainie unceremoniously dumped the contents of her everyday purse into the Sunday one and zipped it shut.

Grabbing her umbrella from the hall closet as she passed, Rainie walked as quickly as possible to her car, remembering with every step why she disliked heels. Already her feet hurt and her ankles were wobbly. Rainie had been a tomboy all her life, and she only wore heels when it was an absolute necessity. She laughed as she imagined what Marla's mother would say if Rainie showed up in tennis shoes.

The air hung heavy with unshed rain, and the day had become as dark and gloomy as early evening. Thunder mumbled in the distance, but still the rain didn't come. Even Rainie, who usually enjoyed storms, was apprehensive.

The small church where Bob and Marla were to be married was on Lupine's main street, and when Rainie arrived, she was pleased to find there weren't many cars in the parking lot. She had thought she was later than she apparently was. Rainie recognized Bob's car and that of Marla's parents, as well as Betty Franks's, the other bridesmaid. The others she assumed belonged to the preacher and the organist.

Rainie parked near the side door and hurried inside. She had seldom been in the church on a Saturday, and it seemed odd that there were no children scampering about or couples gossiping in the halls between services.

Marla had reserved the Sunday school room nearest the sanctuary for her dressing room, and Rainie knew she'd find the bride there. She fully expected to find things in a last-minute turmoil and she wasn't disappointed.

"I'm so glad you're here!" Marla said as she hugged Rainie in a rustle of white satin and stiff lace. Whispering frantically, she added, "My mother is driving me crazy!"

Rainie understood. Mrs. Cane was the sort who would fray nerves much steadier than those of a bride's. "I'll take care of it," she whispered back. Turning to the gray-haired woman, Rainie said, "Mrs. Cane, can you help me get my hat on? I never can seem to do it right."

Mrs. Cane plucked a small blue hat, dyed to match the dresses, out of a milliner's box. "You girls are something else," she complained. "When I was growing up, all girls knew how to put on a hat."

Rainie sat on a chair and let the woman fuss over her. Marla had been a child born late in her parents' lives, and Mrs. Cane teetered between resentment toward her daughter and overprotectiveness.

Out of the corner of her eye, Rainie could see Betty billowing the layers of lace so they would lay smoothly over Marla's train. Eva Jean Massey was there, as well, brushing the hair of the protesting flower girl, one of Marla's cousins. A woman about the same age as Mrs. Cane was tripping nervously about the room, generally getting in everyone's way.

"Aunt Sophie," Marla said to the woman. "Wouldn't you be happier if you went out and sat with Dad?"

"Men are useless at a time like this," Aunt Sophie chirped. "I'll stay here and help you."

"Marla," her mother said, "I told you I would help you with your train if you'll just give me a chance. Rainie, stop fidgeting. Now your hat's crooked again."

As if things weren't already hectic, the door opened and the organist peeped in. "Bad news," she said. "The soloist just called. She's had to cancel out."

"What?" The question came from every direction.

"Her car won't start, and she lives nearly halfway between here and Roan Oak. She says it's coming a flood and an electrical storm, and she has a sore throat anyway."

"She can't do that!" Marla exclaimed.

"Sorry. I'm afraid she has," the organist said. "Even if she left at once she wouldn't get here in time. Guests are already coming in."

"I'll kill her!" Marla promised. "I'll wring her neck with my bare hands!"

"Hush, Marla," Mrs. Cane commanded. "You'll do no such thing. Sophie, you sing beautifully. You take her place."

Aunt Sophie looked up expectantly. "Of course, Hattie. Whatever you say."

Marla was making a visible effort not to groan. "Mother, I don't need a soloist. Really I don't."

"Nonsense. Sophie was singing at weddings before you were born. Sophie, go find the sheet music."

As the little woman obediently left, Marla threw Rainie an imploring look.

"Mrs. Cane, I think Marla's right about not—"

"There," the older woman interrupted. "Your hat is pinned on, and if you don't knock it off again, it will be just fine. As for Sophie, she was hurt that she hadn't been asked to sing at her only niece's wedding, and this a much better arrangement."

"Yes, ma'am," Rainie said. She'd always found Mrs. Cane intimidating.

Mrs. Cane bustled around her daughter giving well-intentioned but ego-deflating instructions like, "Hold in your stomach," and "Quit slouching," and "You're wearing entirely too much makeup. Where did you ever find eye shadow in that strange shade of blue?"

By the time the wedding party was lined up in the vestibule outside the sanctuary, Marla was practically in tears, and both Rainie and Betty were gritting their teeth. When Mrs. Cane was finally escorted down to the front pew, everyone sighed with relief. Everyone except Marla's father, who was standing next to his daughter looking as if he were attending a funeral instead of a wedding. As the organist was given the signal that the bride was ready, the flower girl was handed a basket of rose petals, which she promptly dropped. As the processional music rang out, Rainie and Betty scrambled to refill the basket and send the little girl on her way.

As Rainie went down the aisle, she couldn't help but think of her own wedding. She, too, had come to the altar in clouds of white, and Harry, like Bob, had looked nervous enough to faint dead away on the spot. The altar was scented with banks of flowers and tiers of slim, white candles, and the minister looked happier than the bride's and groom's parents to see them wed. Rainie only hoped Marla and Bob would be one of the lucky couples who would stay happy together.

She watched with pride as her friend Marla, now smiling radiantly, walked with measured steps down the aisle. Would she and Lucas ever make this commitment? Rainie wondered. All at once it seemed to be such a great deal to ask. She had been wrong about marriage once, and it had ended in divorce. Could she ever again promise to love and honor someone forever? Even if it were Lucas? The flowers trembled in Rainie's hand as she took the bridal bouquet from Marla.

Marla's father made the appropriate response in giving the bride away, while Bob stepped up beside his bride. Rainie had never seen a man look so nervous, and she smiled with affection. There was something awesome and touching and springlike about any wedding, just as there was in a birth. Endless possibilities lay ahead—joys, heartaches, children. All the shared times that made up a marriage. Marla and Bob would still be individuals, but now they would also be a unit.

As Rainie turned her attention back to the proceedings, she heard the minister leading Bob in a recitation of his wedding vows, and with each phrase, Bob seemed to be gathering courage. As soon as the matching wedding bands were exchanged, the organist began to play and Aunt Sophie burst into song. Rainie had never heard the woman sing, as Sophie attended Lupine's other church, and she had to struggle to suppress a giggle for the woman had an enthusiastic billygoat contralto that was half a beat behind and a quarter note off-key. Following the song, the newlyweds kissed, and Marla threw Rainie an I-told-you-so look as she swept up the aisle on her new husband's arm.

Rainie fell into step with the best man and followed the couple out.

The reception was held in the fellowship hall in the basement of the church. Everyone in the small town seemed to have turned out to wish Bob and Marla a happy marriage. Small boys and girls dodged in and out of the crowd, and every so often a laugh or an exclamation rose above the general murmur of the well-wishers.

Aunt Sophie joined the others with the air of a diva consorting with the public and accepted praises for her musical accomplishments. The flower girl ate too many pieces of cake and drank too much punch and announced that she was about to be sick. As Mrs. Cane flitted about inspecting things, she noted the caterer had used pale pink roses on the groom's cake instead of yellow ones and that the punch bowl had a chip on its lip.

"It's a wonderful wedding," Rainie said to Marla, who stood hand in hand with Bob. "Lupine will talk about it for weeks."

Marla laughed as her mother stormed by to call the catering company and demand a refund. "Mother is in her element."

"So is your Aunt Sophie."

"At least it's over," Bob said philosophically. "When can we leave?"

"As soon as I change." Marla stood on tiptoes and lightly kissed him. "I'll be right back."

Rainie helped Marla change from her wedding gown to a going-away dress of royal blue. As they were heading back to the fellowship hall Rainie put her hand on her friend's arm and stopped her for a moment. "Marla, be happy."

Marla smiled and patted Rainie's hand. "We will be."

Everyone looked up expectantly as Marla entered, and Betty handed her the wedding bouquet. The bride turned her back to the crowd and tossed the flowers over her shoulder. They landed neatly in Betty's arms.

Rainie saw the woman's face flush pink, and Betty grinned at her steady boyfriend who responded with a wink. Then Bob grabbed Marla's hand, and they rushed for the door. Everyone hurried after them, and amid a shower of rice from well-wishers, the newly married couple dashed across the church lawn and into Bob's car. Rainie waved with the others until the car was out of sight.

"Our baby's gone."

Rainie turned to see Mrs. Cane groping blindly for her husband's hand. To her surprise there were tears in the woman's eyes. Rainie had never suspected Mrs. Cane to be a person to exhibit tenderness.

"He had better be good to her," Mr. Cane said darkly.

Rainie turned away. She helped Mrs. Cane and Sophie gather up Marla's wedding dress and veil, and luckily they were able to get them into the Cane's car before the first heavy drops of rain began to fall. Rainie hurried back into the church to get her purse and barely reached her car before the heavens opened. Flashes of lightning were followed quickly by booming thunder as she made her way through town. Her wipers shoved sheets of water off the windshield, and she had to lean forward, straining to see the turns that led to her house.

After a treacherous drive, Rainie pulled into her yard, greatly relieved that she'd arrived safely. Thinking the storm would let up soon, she waited for a while, but at length gave up and decided she'd have to make a dash for the house. She slipped off her heels, for they were useless to run in, and wriggled out of her panty hose. Setting her shoes and hose aside, she drew a deep breath and jumped out of the car, snapping open her umbrella as she began sprinting for the house. The wind immediately turned the umbrella inside out, and by the time she reached her back porch, she was drenched.

Dripping and cold, her feet muddy to the ankles, she stepped onto the vinyl flooring of her kitchen and sighed at the mess she was making. Without turning on the lights, she stripped to the skin and hung her soaked clothing on the hooks that she used for slickers and rainwear, then hurried to her bathroom where she took a hot shower. After toweling herself dry, she dressed in jeans and a red sweater and went back to the kitchen and made herself a cup of instant coffee.

As she stood looking out at the rain, Rainie became aware that something didn't feel right. She thought of the mare and wondered if maybe something was wrong in the barn. Billy and Oscar would have left at least an hour ago.

Finishing off her coffee, Rainie decided it wouldn't hurt her to get wet again. At least this time she'd be better prepared, and she knew she wouldn't be able to rest as long as she had this nagging worry.

She donned her heavy rubber boots, shrugged into her yellow slicker and pulled the hood close about her face. Tak-

ing a deep breath, she waited until she saw a flash of lighting, then ran out into the storm as thunder reverberated off
the mountains. By the time lightning blazed again, she was
safe inside the barn.

9

LUCAS GRINNED and let his hands rest on either side of the typewriter. The first chapter—the one he considered to be the most difficult in every book—was done. It was finished and it was good. When he had first started writing, he had had little objectivity, but having written so many books since, he now had a feel for whether a chapter worked or not. His writer's block was over and his work was through for the day.

He stood up and stretched to relieve the muscle tension in his shoulders and felt his back pop. A glance at his watch revealed it was almost suppertime. The hours had passed quickly as they always did when he was busy with a story.

A rumble of thunder drew his attention, and from his living-room window he could see that it was raining; he had been so engrossed in his work, he hadn't noticed. He stepped out onto the porch for a better view of the gentle, silver rain falling onto his wildflower-strewn meadow. The long puddles that had formed beneath the drip line of his roof indicated it had been raining for a while. Thunder resounded, rolling through the valleys of the distant mountain as the storm moved away. The rain smelled fresh and sweet; the whole world was pleasant. His writer's block was over. More important than that, he was in love.

Lucas leaned against one of the porch supports and put his hands in his jeans' pockets. Loving Rainie was easy; deciding what to do about it was hard. He couldn't ask her to give up her way of life and move to Memphis, especially knowing how she felt about cities and her first marriage, in which she had evidently had little say in anything. Could he be happy living in the mountains? While Lucas didn't live as high, wide, and handsome as Jordan Lane was purported to, he still enjoyed diversions and nightlife. Lupine offered neither. But Lupine had Rainie.

He wanted to see her, rain or no rain. Going inside, he pulled on a jean jacket over his blue chambray shirt. Over that he put on the lightweight oiled poncho that had hung in the closet for years. Then he went to saddle the horse.

As Lucas rode Red out of the barn, he felt as if he and his novel's hero were kindred spirits. Living in a cabin with no electricity and riding a horse to court his sweetheart gave him a link with the pioneer family that he would never have found in his house in Memphis. He could almost imagine Rainie as the woman in gingham who churned butter and foraged for wild berries and won the hero's heart. The idea of Rainie churning brought a wide smile to his face, for domesticity wasn't her long suit, but that wasn't important. Even Lupine sold ready-made butter.

Red, an easygoing horse who didn't care whether he was in the rain or not, made his way carefully down the wet slope. The distant thunder didn't faze him at all. Lucas, who could handle far more spirited horses than Red, was glad to be able to enjoy the ride and not have to work with the animal. He liked Red's amiable disposition.

The mountain was clean and sweet-scented from the passing storm. The rain made an elemental music as it splashed from tree to bush to grass. Lucas thought if silver had a sound, it would be that of the rain.

Rainie was like the mountain, he thought. Ever-changing and always with a new vista to intrigue him. Just as he never knew exactly what he would see along the familiar woodland trails, he never knew quite what to expect from her. Despite her mercurial quality, he suspected she was also as constant as the mountains. Rainie, once she gave her heart, would be true. That was evident in the way she had given eight years to a marriage that must have been a mistake from the start. Lucas had that same constancy.

He shook his head. What was he thinking of? He couldn't ask Rainie to marry him. She thought he was a backwoods hermit and had fallen in love with him as such. What would she think if he suddenly became Jordan Lane? His reputation for being a playboy was such that she would probably believe he had been playing her for a fool. As easily as Rainie jumped to conclusions, she was certain to think that. He was, at present, in the unique position of knowing that this woman genuinely cared for him as a person and not because of his image as Jordan Lane. But Rainie had said Jordan Lane was her favorite author, and to him that implied that she probably knew of his media-generated reputation and surely had formed an opinion about Jordan Lane based on that knowledge. Learning his true identity would have to affect their relationship.

He let himself through the gate, and as he rode toward Rainie's orchard, the rain picked up again and he could feel it penetrating the old poncho. He urged Red to quicken his pace, and was thankful to find the barn door open. Without slowing, he rode Red into the welcome shelter. As he dismounted, a voice from the back of the barn startled him.

"Lucas! I didn't expect you to come in weather like this."

He looked in the direction of the voice, pleasantly surprised that Rainie was there. "I wanted to see you. What are you doing out here?"

She turned back to the stall. "It's the mare. She's in labor. Of all the times she could have picked, this is the worst. Bob and Marla were married today and have already left on their honeymoon. The storm has flooded the hollow between here and Oscar's house, and he can't get here until the water goes down, and that probably won't be until tomorrow. I called Billy, and got no answer." She shook her head in concern. "The mare isn't doing well."

As Lucas approached her, he decided to suppress his urge to pull her into his arms and passionately kiss her. She was clearly preoccupied with her worry about the horse, and he didn't want her to think he was unsympathetic to her plight. There would be time for loving later, when this crisis was passed.

The mare was in the far corner of her stall, her breath coming as quickly as if she had been running, her head hanging low. Now and then she shifted her weight as if she were in pain. "What's wrong? I know she's thin, but horses have colts all the time."

"I know, but something just doesn't feel right. I can't explain it, but I know she's in trouble."

"Let me unsaddle Red, and I'll be back with you."

Rainie leaned on the top rail of the stall, trying to recall all she knew about birthings, but her knowledge was sparse. Although she had lived around horses most of her life, she had only bred them for two years. There had rarely been any complications, and never without Bob Pollard being there with all his medical knowledge. He had always known what to do.

"Is there a vet in Roan Oak?" Lucas called to her.

"No, Bob takes care of both towns. There must be one in Millsburg, but that's miles away. I doubt the vet would be willing to come here. Besides, I don't think the mare can wait."

"How long does a horse's labor last?"

"It varies. But she's not healthy, and I think she started this morning. Since Billy and Oscar assumed she wasn't due for weeks, they didn't realize what was happening. I had so much on my mind, I didn't take a good look at her until I came home

"Go on back and make yourself at home," Rainie said as she soaped her hands at the kitchen sink. "There are towels in the cabinet and soap is in the dish."

As she thawed hamburger patties in the microwave, she heard the shower come on. Lucas fit so well into her life. She liked the idea of him in the shower while she cooked their meal. With Lucas, she didn't mind being a little domestic. Unbidden thoughts of Lucas, naked, his skin slick with water, came to her and she smiled.

She fried the hamburgers while he bathed, and as she was setting the table, she heard him blow-drying his hair. By the time he came into the kitchen, the meal was ready. "It's just hamburgers. Nothing special." He looked so sexy with his freshly shampooed hair and his sleeves rolled loosely back to his elbows.

"I like hamburgers."

"Sit there," she said as she put the food on the table. "Do you want a soft drink or iced tea?"

"Either." He was studying her as if she were doing something special, as if it gave him pleasure to watch her doing anything at all.

They ate in virtual silence, both afraid of saying too much. Rainie was curious about him, but she knew from experience that any questions she asked would be answered vaguely or not at all. She had no idea Lucas was keeping quiet in order not to tell her all there was to know about himself.

After the meal was cleared away, Rainie and Lucas went into the living room and she said, "Would you like a fire? The nights are still so cool and with the rain it'll be cozy."

"Sure." He knelt on the hearth and began to build a fire.

"You do that so well. Not everyone can, you know. I guess it comes from practice."

He fed a log to the fire and didn't answer.

"Why *did* you happen to read a veterinary book?" she asked.

For a minute she thought he hadn't heard her, and she was about to repeat the question when he said, "It was handy that I knew about it. Luckily I have good recall." Then he paused, as if waiting to see if she would ask why he had such a book on hand in the first place.

Instead, Rainie got a quilt off the quilt rack and spread it like a pallet on the floor in front of the hearth. She sat cross-legged on it, basking in the fire's warmth, thoroughly engaged in trying to solve the enigma that was Lucas Dalton. Perhaps, she thought, his resistance to talking about his past came from living alone and having no one to share experiences with, or maybe he was just a private person. She understood a person's right to privacy, yet her mind was filled with questions.

"Why did you leave this morning without telling me goodbye?" He seemed surprised by her question.

"I didn't want to wake you."

"I always get up early."

"Even when you're up most of the night?" he asked.

"I'm never up most of the night. At least not for that reason."

"Never?" His eyes searched her face.

Rainie met his gaze directly. "Never. At least not until you came along."

He smiled as if that was the answer he had wanted to hear.

"How about you?" she asked.

"I'm a . . . hermit. Remember?" For some reason he looked as if he was reluctant to remind her.

"Roan Oak isn't that far away. You said so yourself."

"I'm not interested in anyone in Roan Oak, or anywhere else except here. I love you."

Rainie scanned his features for any sign of duplicity, but found none. "I had hoped you'd meant that last night."

"I'd be a fool to say it if I didn't mean it."

"A lot of people say what they think a person wants to hear."

"Not me." He picked up the poker and pushed the top log of the fire into a better position.

In silence, he settled back beside her on the quilt. The firelight gilded his strong features in a coppery hue and made his hair seem even blacker. He sat with one knee drawn up and his arm resting on it. His gaze was fixed on the blazing fire as if he were in deep contemplation. He could have been thinking of her, or of a dozen other things. She simply couldn't figure him out.

He turned to her and spoke. "I'm not the sort to say I love you unless I mean it," he continued. "I wouldn't hurt you in any way."

"I admire your honesty," she replied. "Of all the people I've ever known, I think you must be the most honest."

"Rainie . . ."

"I admire that."

The fire crackled in the silence and rain drummed against the window.

"What were you going to say?" she asked at last.

"Nothing. Never mind." He looked uncomfortable.

Rainie put her hand on his arm. "I think I understand. You're worried because you let me see how vulnerable you can be. All people in love are like that. Are you afraid I'll expect more than you're willing to give?"

He stared at her without answering.

"I won't ask you to marry me," she said. "I'm not trying to trap you into anything."

To her surprise, he laughed. "What's so funny?" she asked.

"Nothing. It's just that you're the only person I've ever known who can leap to conclusions with such ease."

"What are you talking about? What conclusion?"

He put his arm around her and drew her over so that she leaned across his chest and was cradled in his embrace. "I don't feel trapped. If I did, I wouldn't be here."

"Then what . . . ?"

"Have you ever been in a situation where one thing has led to another and before long it's so out of hand you don't see any way to fix it?"

"No. Have you?"

He looked as though he wanted to reply but couldn't say the words. His eyes were troubled as they searched her face. Rainie thought he must be referring to his broken marriage and remembering the hurt feelings it caused. To ease his pain and get his mind off the subject, she said, "Tom Hanford says there's a suspicious stranger in Roan Oak."

"Tom Hanford?"

"The sheriff in Lupine. He says we should all be careful until he finds out what the man is up to around here."

"That's good advice. And knowing your dogs, I hope you'll keep your doors locked. They wouldn't bark at Jack the Ripper."

"I usually remember to lock them."

"Be sure you do. I don't want anything to happen to you."

She smiled. "You don't? Nothing at all?"

"I can think of one thing," he admitted, "but you'll enjoy it."

Her smile broadened. "Oh?"

He drew her closer and Rainie slipped her arms around his neck as her mouth met his in a tender kiss. His lips were warm from the fire, and his skin smelled of soap. She ran the tip of her tongue over his lips. "You taste good."

"So do you." His voice was deep with emotion. He smoothed his hand up her side and cupped her breast. "You feel good, too." Slowly his fingers moved over the mound of her breast, teasing her body into a response.

Rainie felt her pulse leap in excitement. "You're sexy," she said. "Kind and wonderful and most definitely sexy."

"So are you. It was one of the first things I noticed about you."

"Oh? I'd have said the first thing you noticed was that I was trespassing."

He nibbled at the ticklish part of her neck. "So maybe it was the second thing I noticed. I'm sure it was one of the top two." He shifted his position so that she lay beneath him. "You're like no one I've ever known before."

She put her finger on his lips and traced the line of his mouth and stroked his silky beard. "I can't figure you out," she admitted. "You're a very confusing man."

"I guess we have a lot in common. To say you're complex is an understatement."

"It may take me years to really get to know you." She watched him draw back, and it was as if a veil had fallen behind his eyes. "Did I say something wrong?"

"No." He smiled at her and gently repeated, "No, you didn't say anything wrong."

Rainie unbuttoned his shirt and stroked the firm muscles of his chest. "I love your body. You look as if you regularly work out in a gym." The notion of a gym room in his cabin was amusing, but the smile on her face was one of appreciation of his magnificent physique.

Lucas's smiling dark eyes searched hers.

"I guess it comes from living with such few conveniences," she answered for him as she drew his shirt to one side, then traced lazy circles on his chest. "Nice," she sighed. "So nice."

Lucas removed her clothing as she removed his, taking his
time and savoring every inch of her newly exposed flesh.
Soon they lay on the quilt with nothing between them but
their love. The fire kissed their bare skins, and at Rainie's
urging, Lucas rolled onto his back and she positioned herself
above him. "I want to always remember you like this," she
said. "Looking at me the way you are with your skin hot from
the fire."

"It's not only the fire," he told her. "You have a lot to do
with it." He laced his fingers in her hair. "I was thinking the
same thing about you. Your lips are soft from my kisses and
I see love shining in your eyes. Your skin is the golden hue of
rich cream, and your lips and nipples are the same deep shade
of coral."

Rainie caught her breath at the loving in his words. "You
have the soul of a poet."

"No," he said with one of his mysterious smiles. "Not a
poet."

She bent and kissed him, her lips parting as his tongue
sought hers. Her body molded to his and her pale breasts
mounded against his chest. His kisses left her breathless and
wanting more. Desire flamed deep within her, spreading like
wildfire throughout her body.

As rain blew against the window and the fire burned
brightly on the hearth, Rainie enjoyed the touch of his hands
and lips and matched him pleasure for pleasure. With Lucas,
she felt no need to hold back her desires. He met her passion
with greater passion, and together they found new ways of
giving and prolonging the ecstasy of their lovemaking.

When she could wait no longer, Rainie eased her body onto
his, making them one, and he arched himself against her. His
eyes were black with desire, and she knew her own expression mirrored his need. She moistened her kiss-swollen lips

with the tip of her tongue, and moving seductively, she drew their ecstasy to a higher pitch.

Lucas covered her breasts with his palms then rolled both her nipples between his thumbs and forefingers. Rainie moaned as his caresses sent shock waves directly to the center of her being. He knew instinctively how to touch her and how to give her the greatest pleasure. Her breasts swayed against his hands as she rocked her hips.

Raising his upper body, he captured one of her nipples in his mouth. Rainie let her head roll back, and closed her eyes as the ecstasy of his loving consumed her. Soon she felt her body quicken, and her hips increased their rhythm. Suddenly she reached her fulfillment and cried out as wave after hot wave rushed through her. Lucas was the center of her universe, and nothing existed but the two of them.

Gradually the pulsing pleasure began to subside, and when she opened her eyes, he was watching her.

"I've never known anyone could be so responsive," he said. "You were made to love and be loved."

"I was made for you," she murmured as he began to move in her again. "And you were made for me."

This time the ecstasy raced through her more quickly than before, as if her body were so hungry for his that it could never be satisfied. Rainie had heard of multiple climaxes, but before Lucas, she had never known such joy. She was sure her life would never be the same again.

When her desire leapt again to his urging, she nudged him and together they rolled over, putting him on top. His black hair fell over his forehead in an unruly thatch, and his muscles bunched and rippled as he expertly stroked her. His hard flesh drove her higher and higher, and just when she thought she would explode, he stopped and remained perfectly motionless for a moment. When he moved again, a climax, more intense than any of the others, tore through her, and this time she knew he was experiencing his own, as well.

As they lay in a lover's embrace, breathing in unison, the world slowly reformed about them. The fire was burning low, and the logs were melting into glowing embers. The storm had moved away down the valley, and only a gentle rain fell on the peaked roof. Rainie had never known such peace nor such pleasure.

"I'm glad I fell in love with you," she said as she stroked her fingers along the pulse that beat steadily in his neck. "I don't think being in love with anyone else would be nearly as wonderful."

He was silent for a long time. "Wouldn't you feel the same about me if I were somebody else? If I were rich and famous, for instance."

She laughed softly. "If you were rich and famous, you wouldn't be lying here on a quilt in my living room." She had never met anyone famous and almost no one who was really rich. Since moving to Lupine, she had narrowed her chances of ever meeting anyone like that to the infinitesimal. Although she didn't know anyone like that, she was sure no one rich and famous would deliver a foal or make love on the floor, much less be anything at all like Lucas. She rubbed her cheek on his shoulder. "I love you exactly the way you are. I wouldn't want you to be different in any way."

Lucas caressed her hair as he thought about what she had said. He couldn't risk telling her the truth. If he did so, he might lose the only woman he had ever really loved. Instead he kissed her.

"Promise me something," she said.

"What?"

"Promise me that when I wake up in the morning, you'll be here."

He kissed her soft hair above her forehead, his beard tickling her nose. "What about Billy and Oscar? I don't want to embarrass you."

"Tomorrow is Sunday. They don't work then."

"In that case, I'll be here."

She lifted her head and looked into his eyes. "Is that why you left so early?"

He smiled and stroked the back of his fingers over the curve of her cheek.

She laid her head back down on his shoulder. "I knew you were wonderful."

He didn't answer.

10

"I LOVE to wake up beside you," Rainie said as she cuddled against Lucas's side and planted a string of kisses across his chest.

He drew the covers up over her bare shoulder and intertwined his fingers in her hair. "You're even beautiful in the morning. Especially with that look in your eyes."

"How do I look?" She put her hand on his chest and rested her chin on it.

"Like a woman in love."

Her smile was sweet. "I do love you."

"I love you, Rainie."

For a long moment they lay there savoring the luxury of being together and of their blossoming love, and it was with reluctance that Rainie said, "I think we ought to go check on the colt."

Lucas nodded. "We should."

Happiness sang in her to hear him count them as "we." They had greeted the dawn with their lovemaking, and that had been hours ago. "I'm glad you kept your promise and stayed all night."

"I'll always keep my promises to you. I don't ever want to see you hurt or disappointed."

"As if you could ever disappoint me," she scoffed with a laugh. "I may not always understand you, but I know you pretty well now. After these past two nights, I certainly should."

He only smiled.

"Do you eat breakfast?"

"Not usually. If you know me so well, why don't you know the answer to that?" he teased.

"I know *you*. I just don't know everything about you. The details will come later. The important thing is that I know who you are in here." She tapped the area over his heart.

"Do you?"

"I love you. And miracle of miracles, you love me in return. Nothing else is important."

"It could be."

"Not to me." She rolled out of bed and walked gracefully to her closet. The morning sunlight creamed her naked body with a pearly luster and brought out reddish highlights in her dark hair. "Are you going to lay in bed all day, or do you want to go see the colt with me?"

"I was just admiring the view," he said with a grin. "I'm glad you don't object to my looking at you. You're beautiful. A cross between a pixie and a Lorelei."

"You're going to spoil me. I'm not used to such compliments."

"You'll have to get used to them, because I'm not going to stop. Your hair is like a cobweb of night with sunshine tangled in it. I've seen your eyes in fields of wildflowers and never knew they were hinting of you until you rode into my life. Your laughter is the sound of sunbeams."

Rainie looked at him with a puzzled expression. "How can you think of such beautiful things to say?"

"You inspire me."

"Hermits are vastly underrated. If the word ever gets out that you're all so poetical, none of you will be left alone."

He sobered. "I wish you didn't think of me as a hermit. Is it really that important to you?"

"Of course it is, since it made you the way you are. We're all the sum total of our experiences. You said before you didn't object to the term 'hermit.' I didn't mean to offend you."

"Couldn't you think of me as merely someone who lives alone? Hermit sounds so antisocial."

"Well, aren't you? Otherwise why would you have tried so hard to get rid of me?"

He swung his long legs over the edge of the bed and started dressing. "Maybe because you were being a pest."

"There's no need for you to pretend to be brusque." She zipped her jeans and went to a drawer to get a bra. "I can see right through you."

He grinned. "It's a shame you can't go around dressed like that all the time. I'm not sure I could ever argue with you."

"That's good to know. The next time you're being impossible, I'll know what to do." She glanced over at him and smiled mischievously. "Let's hope we aren't in public at the time."

In short order they finished dressing and headed for the barn. The sun overhead was brilliant, and the world had been washed clean by the storm. Birds sang in celebration of life and spring and wildflowers bloomed in swaths of color in the pastures. "I love spring," Rainie said. "It's so full of promise."

Lucas looped his arm over her shoulder as they gazed at the colt and mare. Both were bright-eyed and alert. As Rainie had said, the colt was a true red with the black markings of a blood-bay. A large white star dominated his forehead. Even though not yet a day old, he was frisky on his spindly legs and curious about everything.

"He's surprisingly pretty," Lucas said. "He must take after his papa."

"The mare will look good once she fattens up. This time next year you won't recognize her."

Lucas looked down at Rainie. "A lot can happen in a year."

Rainie felt a touch of apprehension, but refused to let it take root. She was too happy to let worry come in. "Want some coffee? I seldom eat breakfast, but I become a bear without caffeine."

"Sure. I wouldn't turn down coffee."

Hand in hand they went back to the house. Rainie switched on the radio on her kitchen countertop as she filled two coffee cups with tap water. The station was one that played continuous music except for brief news reports on the hour and half hour. Lucas took a seat at her table.

"I can hardly wait for Bob to get back," Rainie said as she put the cups in the microwave. "I'm really going to rub it in about the colt. I think I'll tell him you and I are going into competition with him by opening a veterinary maternity clinic."

"Bob knows about me?"

She thought a minute. "I can't remember if I mentioned you to him or not. I've told Marla I'm seeing you, and of course Billy and Oscar know." His body tensed, and his smile disappeared. "Shouldn't I have told them?"

"I would rather you hadn't." He was afraid Rainie would feel even more foolish when she learned his true identity, if she had told all her friends he was a reclusive mountain man. Who would ever understand his need for anonymity and solitude as he worked through his writer's block? Her friends were likely to think he was playing a cruel joke on her.

"Why not?"

He shrugged. This didn't seem to be the right time to tell her. He wanted to enjoy her unabashed love for a little while longer.

Rainie took the coffee cups from the microwave and added a spoonful of instant coffee to each. Thoughtfully she said,

"Did I mention the sheriff said I should be on the lookout for a stranger?"

"Yes, you mentioned that. Do you have any milk for the coffee?"

She took a carton out of the refrigerator and gave it to him. "Have you always had that beard?"

He was startled by her question. Was she beginning to realize who he was? His picture, beardless, was on several of his book jackets, and he had noticed one of them on the table beside a comfortable-looking chair in her living room where she apparently sat to read. With a disarming smile he said, "Not always. I couldn't grow a beard at all until I was into puberty."

"How tall are you?"

"Six foot two. Why all the questions?"

"I just wondered."

The radio switched from music to the news. The announcer began on the top news story—the kidnapping of Jordan Lane. "The famous author has been missing for several weeks now," he said, "and the police are baffled. According to Lane's housekeeper—"

Lucas rose from his seat to turn up the volume, but Rainie got to the radio first and snapped it off. "Who needs news on a day like today?" she asked in a voice that sounded a bit too bright and cheerful.

He frowned as he sat back down. Jordan Lane kidnapped? Where had anyone gotten that idea? He wondered if this was another crackpot scheme from his publicist. But surely the man wouldn't do something like this without clearing it first—not something as extreme as reporting a kidnapping.

"More coffee?" she asked.

"I haven't touched this cup yet." He looked away from Rainie toward the window as he took a sip, hoping to hide his troubled thoughts. Why would his housekeeper think he had been kidnapped? He had left her a note saying he was going to the cabin. Hadn't he? His decision to leave town had been a spur of the moment one, but he remembered writing a note. What had he done with it? "Mind if I turn the radio back on?"

"In a minute." She yanked the plug out of the wall and examined the prongs. "Do you think these are making good contact?"

"They were before you unplugged it."

"It sounded like it had a lot of static in it to me." She fiddled with the prongs as if wiggling them would solve the problem. "You know, it seems funny you would ask for milk for your coffee when you don't have a refrigerator. Wouldn't you ask for powdered creamer, if that's what you're used to using?"

"What?" His mind was on more important matters than how he drank his coffee. "Right. Say, Rainie, I have to be going." He got up from the table.

"Now? This minute?"

"There's something I forgot to do." He hoped she wouldn't try to pin him down because he was no good at lying. What *had* he done with that note to his housekeeper? He stepped closer and lightly kissed her cheek, not noticing that she flinched. "See you later."

As Rainie stared after him, she slowly raised her hand and touched her cheek where he had kissed her.

As Lucas rode up the mountain, he struggled to remember the details of the night he had left Memphis. Surely he hadn't been so absentminded as to forget to leave the note explaining where he had gone. But it was possible. When he left Memphis, he had had little on his mind but his writer's block.

He freed Red in the pen and went to the cabin. Jordan Lane kidnapped! Who had put out a story like that? He decided if it was his publicist, this would be the last straw. The story about his "engagement" to the daughter of a billionaire sheikh had almost destroyed his social life. At least that lie hadn't dealt with anything illegal. Kidnapping was a federal crime, and the FBI had no sense of humor. Lucas wondered if he could be in a legal jam over this.

He went directly to the sport coat he had worn on his exodus from the city, and hurriedly searched it. In the inside pocket, he found a crisp sheet of folded paper. "Damn!"

He glared down at the note. Now he remembered. Just as he finished writing the note, the phone rang. Evidently he had absentmindedly folded it and stuffed it into his pocket. No wonder everyone was upset!

Without hesitation, Lucas set about to correct the mistake. In his office, he rolled a sheet of paper into his typewriter and typed a quick note to his agent, Aaron Tavish.

Jordan Lane is alive and well and hidden in the mountains where no one can find him. Call off the search and relax. I'll be in touch soon.

He re-read the note to be sure it was clear. There was no need to go into greater detail. Aaron was his friend and he knew all about the cabin. This would reassure him, and Aaron could see to it that everyone else understood. Lucas's reprieve from writer's block was still too tenuous for him to risk leaving the cabin as yet. Once a story started unfolding, he was almost superstitious about doing anything to change the mood of his writing. He would stay in seclusion until the rough draft was finished.

RAINIE STILL FELT the brush of his beard across her skin from Lucas's parting kiss as she watched him cross the yard to the barn. Her hands and feet were as cold as ice, and the hair prickled on the back of her neck as she stared after him.

Could *he* be the stranger Tom had warned her against? But he had always lived on the mountain. He was local! He was also a recluse so everyone might not know that. Tom had said the stranger was unfriendly, and Lucas had certainly acted that way toward her at first.

With trembling fingers she plugged the radio back into the outlet and turned the dial in search of another news report, but all she found was music and church services. She switched it off. Had he noticed what the announcer was saying about Jordan Lane? He must have because he had reached out as if to turn it off himself.

Rainie felt nauseated. Lucas a kidnapper? Impossible! She might fall in love with a penniless hermit, but never with a kidnapper!

As she watched, Lucas rode out of the barn and galloped away. He was certainly in a rush to leave.

She went to the phone and dialed the first three digits of the sheriff's number, then her fingers tightened on the receiver. Screwing her eyes shut, she drew a trembling breath and hung up. Lucas was no kidnapper! She couldn't possibly tell Tom that he was. She loved Lucas.

She looked back out the window, but Lucas was gone from sight. Deep in thought, she aimlessly wandered into her bedroom and sat on her bed. In an almost dreamlike state of bewilderment, she turned her head and stared at the place where Lucas had slept beside her and where they had made love only hours before. Lucas a kidnapper? It couldn't be!

With cold hands she picked up his pillow and wadded it into her lap. As she hugged it she tried to think rationally. He couldn't be a kidnapper because she had been in his cabin and no one else had been there. If Jordan Lane was tied up in a corner she would certainly have noticed him. True, she had only seen the main room, but no kidnapper would be so stupid as to invite a guest for dinner with his victim tied up in the next room.

And Lucas certainly didn't fit the profile of a criminal. He was gentle and a tender lover. His initial brusqueness had only been a facade. The past two nights had proved that.

She stood up and put the pillow back on the bed. Lucas was no kidnapper. She was being foolish, jumping to conclusions again. How could she love someone and think such a horrible thing about him? The idea made her feel guilty and unworthy of his love. Lucas had the soul of a poet. He loved her; she loved him. He deserved an apology, and then they could laugh at her foolishness—and he could explain why he had acted so peculiarly when he heard the news brief about Jordan Lane being kidnapped.

Rainie went into the kitchen and turned on the oven. The best way she knew to apologize was with chocolate. She took out her recipe box and flipped through it for her favorite recipe for chocolate cake.

LUCAS PUT THE LETTER to Aaron Tavish in an envelope with the agent's name and address typed on the front, then tossed it onto the kitchen table. When he finished writing for the day, he would take it down to Rainie and ask her to post it in her mailbox.

Going back into his office, he inserted a sheet of paper in the typewriter and sat down to write. Almost at once the story of the two families, one on the top of the mountain and the other on the slope, resumed in his imagination where he had left off the day before. As usual, he lost himself in the writing and seemed to be actually living through the tale as an unseen observer. This was the time when writing was good and his career seemed worth all the hard work. The between-book letdowns and the laborious revisions were worth enduring in order to experience the escape into his world of fantasy with the first draft of every new book. Lucas felt like a time traveler who wasn't creating the story so much as witnessing it. The hours passed quickly.

At noon Lucas stopped and flexed his muscles. He was at the end of a scene, and it was a natural place to take a break. After lunch he would finish the chapter and go back to Rainie.

He went into the kitchen and made himself two sandwiches. From the cool cellar he got a canned soft drink and went out onto his porch. The day was beautiful. He imagined the earth had been created just so days like this could happen.

It was too pretty a day to stay at the cabin, so Lucas crossed the meadow and went into the forest. At once the air was cooler, and he smelled the earthy scent of loamy dirt and the fragrance of the pines. White hepatica and pale pink purslane were scattered about, and he had to watch his step to avoid crushing the delicate clusters of rue anemone and trillium. Birds flitted through the treetops overhead, and the sun spangled the forest floor through breaks in the umbrellas of leaves.

Lucas stepped into a familiar clearing and looked about in satisfaction. Sumac, with its flowers still white and tinged with pale green, dotted a field of yarrow and orange milkweed. Red, tube-shaped clematis wound over the weathered remains of an old log fence. Lucas occasionally came here at dawn and dusk to watch for deer in the clearing.

He sat on a sun-warmed rock and balanced his canned drink beside him. Yellow butterflies skipped in the air above the nodding flowers, and he could hear a honeybee nearby. As he ate, he compared this place to the view from his house in Memphis, and decided this was better. Lucas loved the mountains, especially since he had found Rainie.

Would he be happy here? Permanently? He imagined Rainie as his wife and two, maybe three, children, all of whom had her deep blue eyes. This would be a good place to bring up a family, he thought. There was plenty of fresh air and horses to ride and dogs to pet, and not a street gang or drug pusher for miles. Lupine probably didn't have the greatest of school systems, but as a writer, Lucas would be home with the children, and with his extensive, personal library, he could tutor them to supplement what they would learn in the Lupine schools. He almost laughed aloud at his fancy. Here he was planning which books to read to his children, and he wasn't even engaged to their mother-to-be.

Rainie would probably accept if he proposed. She hadn't mentioned marriage, but he knew she loved him. He had never felt so loved in his entire life. But she loved Lucas Dalton, not Jordan Lane.

With a sigh, he took another bite of his sandwich. When he told her who he was, she was bound to change toward him—he had seen it too often. After waiting so long to tell her, she might be too angry to see him again. She might decide she preferred the kind of life Jordan Lane was assumed to lead. Lucas loved Rainie, but he had to admit he didn't know her very well.

RAINIE WALKED UP the slope of the mountain, carrying the freshly baked cake in a plastic container. She felt foolish for having thought for a minute that Lucas could be involved in anything illegal. Once again her overactive imagination had carried her away.

As she stepped into Lucas's cabin clearing, she noted how truly picturesque the setting was. His cabin could easily be a cottage in a picture book, she thought. If she lived here, she would plant flowers around the porch and at the base of the house, but she wouldn't touch the meadow. The wildflowers made a carpet more lovely than manicured grass. Red was in the feed lot, his head hanging over the fence as he watched her. The horse was perfect for Lucas, and she was glad he had accepted the animal.

Somewhat surprised that Lucas didn't come out to meet her, Rainie went up onto the porch and knocked. The door swayed open at her touch. "Lucas?" she called. "Are you here?"

The cabin was silent, so she called again, loudly enough that if he were asleep in the other room he would hear her. Still she got no answer. She pulled the door closed and started to leave, but it seemed silly to take the cake all the way home and have to bring it back later. Surely Lucas wouldn't mind if she came in and left it on the table. Hesitantly she pushed open the door and stepped inside.

The house felt empty without Lucas there and much too quiet. The thought of how Lucas's personality seemed to fill a room brought a smile to her lips. She was glad she had fallen in love with him.

She set the cake on his kitchen table and removed the cover so he would see it as soon as he came into the cabin. As she rotated it so its best side was toward the door, she noticed a letter on the table next to it, and she absently read the name and address. "Aaron Tavish, 300 Fifth Avenue, New York."

Fifth Avenue? How could Lucas possibly know anyone on Fifth Avenue in New York when he never went farther from the mountain than the library at the county seat?

"Lucas?" she called out again. The house was obviously empty.

More out of curiosity than nosiness, she went to the door in the back wall and opened it. Her heart softened at her first view of Lucas's bedroom. No other room could be so personal as the one where he slept and dressed and had his retreat. The neatly made bed was covered with a homespun spread, and a braided rug warmed the pine floor. The two outside walls were chinked logs, but the inner ones, painted a deep blue, were adorned with two paintings—one of a seashore on a foggy day, the other of a mountain forest in an early morning haze. Both scenes were of exceptional quality, and she couldn't imagine them having been done by a relative, but where else could he have gotten them?

As Rainie wandered back into the main room, she debated whether or not to wait for him. Since he had no refrigerator, it was likely that he had to make frequent trips to the store in Roan Oak for perishable goods, and thus she assumed that was where he had gone.

Taking her time, she walked around the room, looking at the things Lucas owned and touched daily. There were several carved animals that were as lifelike as any she had seen in expensive shops. One shelf held a small, copper bowl filled with semi-precious stones, many of which were indigenous to the area and had been polished to a luster, and several Indian pots that appeared to be authentic. Here, too, the pictures on his walls were paintings, not inexpensive prints—a fact Rainie hadn't noticed when she had been here earlier, no doubt because she hadn't been looking at anything but Lucas during that meal. Rainie decided Lucas must have several unusually gifted relatives, for he certainly couldn't have afforded to buy all these things.

She looked out the window in hopes of seeing him, but the meadow was still empty. She went back to the kitchen table, and this time her curiosity got the better of her. She picked up the envelope. Who was Aaron Tavish?

As she turned it over in her hands, she noticed it was unsealed. Fifth Avenue certainly seemed to be a ritzy address. How could he have ever met, let alone have become a correspondent with, someone in New York? Three hundred Fifth Avenue sounded like a large place, not a mere office. Surely if it were an office it would read 300 Fifth Avenue, Suite 44 or something like that. The same would be true if it were going to to an apartment. Did Lucas know someone who owned an entire building on Fifth Avenue?

She had too much integrity to take the letter out and read it. That would be snooping. But it seemed to burn her fingers.

Rainie tossed the envelope back onto the table, and when it slid across and hit the cake plate, one corner of the letter protruded.

She paused. Then she tossed it again. On the fourth toss, the letter fell out, and she stared down at it. Her inquisitiveness was too great. By craning her head around to one side, and blowing hard on the fold of paper, she read, "Aaron." She nudged it off the table and onto the floor. After poking at it with the toe of her shoe, the words "Jordan Lane is alive" leapt up at her.

For a moment Rainie was too stunned to move, then she grabbed up the letter and spread it out on the table.

Jordan Lane is alive and well and hidden in the mountains where no one can find him. Call off the search and relax. I'll be in touch soon.

Rainie's mouth went dry and her breath came in shallow gulps. "Jordan Lane is alive..." Her eyes were wide as she read the letter again.

A noise from outside shot fear through her, and the blood drained from her face as she ran to the front window. It was Lucas returning from the woods. Although he was whistling as though nothing was amiss, she knew better. Panic seized her.

She ran back to the table, and with trembling hands managed somehow to stuff the letter back into the envelope. She mustn't let him find her here! She decided to leave by the back door, but there was no back door! Again she hurried to the window, this time peering cautiously for fear he would see her.

Lucas was heading straight toward the door, and she was trapped! But then he veered off toward the feed lot, and Rainie gulped a deep breath. He paused at the fence to pet Red, and as though in answer to her prayer, he turned his back to the cabin's front door. If she hurried, she could slip out before he turned around.

Anxiously she looked about the room. Has she moved anything? Left her mark somehow? *The cake!*

She slammed the lid back on the cake plate and latched it. Not caring whether the cake slid into the side or not, she ran across the room, and after verifying the coast was clear, she cautiously opened the door and stepped out. She closed the door behind her as quietly as she could, scurried down the length of the porch, slipped under the rail and dropped to the ground.

Her heart was racing as she dodged around the corner and flattened herself against the cabin. Shutting her eyes tight, she willed him to go into the house and not to sit on the porch or, worse, to come around the corner.

It seemed like hours, but only minutes later she heard Lucas climbing the steps and crossing the wooden porch. He paused. Rainie felt physically ill. Had she shut the door all the way? Could he see her shadow or her shirt sleeve? Her pulse was pounding so hard, she was surprised her heartbeat wasn't audible.

Finally the sound of his door closing signaled he was inside, and she leaned away from the cabin. She had been planning her strategy and had decided that if she went up the mountain, she could reach the woods without being in view of the front windows. And if he didn't go into his bedroom, he wouldn't be able to see her out back, either.

But had she remembered to shut the bedroom door? She thought she had, but now she wasn't positive. Her only other choice was to stay beside the cabin until dark, but the risk seemed too high. She would have to chance it now.

Rainie forced her rubbery legs to carry her forward. She didn't dare run for fear he might hear her, so she walked as fast as she could, with the cake carrier bumping against her knee.

After what felt like an eternity, she reached the trees and dodged for cover, risking a look behind her. The meadow was empty, and she could see no face at the bedroom window. *Had her escape gone unnoticed?* She tried to remember if she had left the envelope faceup as she had found it, and whether she had put any telltale wrinkles in it as she stuffed the letter back into its envelope.

Her stomach was knotted and her knees threatened to buckle. Lucas was definitely involved with Jordan Lane's kidnapping!

She circled the meadow, keeping well out of sight in the woods. It wouldn't do for Lucas to guess she had been to the cabin and read that letter.

The way through the woods was rough, and briers wrapped around her ankles at every step. A tangle of dog hobble made her detour farther into the woods, but she kept going. She had never been this way before, but the downward slope of the land told her she was going in the right direction.

When she came across the stream that fed Lucas's feed lot and meandered down to her own pasture, she was relieved. As she followed the familiar landmark, she paused now and then to listen and look behind her to see if she was being followed.

Eventually she reached her own fence, and after shoving the cake carrier through ahead of her, Rainie slipped her body between the strands of barbed wire. Once she was on her own property, she felt less threatened. There was no crime in her being on her own land, cake or no cake.

Several minutes later she topped a bare knoll and saw her house and barn. Never had home looked so welcome. Her horses were grazing in the pastures, the sun shining on their black, brown and red coats. Everything here was as it should be. She was safe.

She entered her house through the kitchen door and locked it behind her. This turn of events was more of a shock than her worst nightmare. *Lucas was a kidnapper!*

She dropped the cake carrier onto the counter, leaned over the sink, and splashed cold water on her face. As she toweled herself dry, she felt a little better, but she was still shaking from head to toe. *A kidnapper!*

Suddenly another thought occurred to her, and she abruptly straightened. If Lucas had kidnapped Jordan Lane, where was the victim? A deep frown creased her brow. She had been all over that house, and it had been silent and empty. The only places she hadn't looked were the bathroom and the closet that led off the main room, and the basement, if there was one. If someone had been hidden in there, especially with her calling out for Lucas, he would have been able to make some noise to get her attention.

Maybe Jordan Lane was dead!

Her dread threatened to return, but she shoved it away. Lucas was certainly no murderer! Besides, the letter had clearly stated that Jordan Lane was alive and hidden somewhere. But where? There was no other cabin or outbuilding on Lucas's land nor were there caves in the area. As far as she knew there were also no mines or quarries. No one would hide a kidnapped victim in the open woods.

The barn? No, she had been in there with Lucas. True he had seemed reluctant to let her in, but she had in fact seen it.

Unlike her own barn, there had been no closed tack room, and the hayloft was open on one end so anyone up there would have been visible. There was no place he could have hidden Jordan Lane. Therefore he must be innocent.

Then what had the letter meant?

Rainie opened the cake carrier and unhappily surveyed the remains. In the trip down the mountain, most of the icing had rubbed off onto the sides of the container, and the cake sat off-center on the plate. Slowly she scraped the icing off the container and back onto the cake, then cut herself a slice. Chocolate had always been a solace in times of trial. As she took a bite, the tears that had been gathering in her eyes began to trickle down her cheeks.

LUCAS PAUSED on his porch, looking over at the old road in hopes of seeing Rainie. All the way back from the clearing where he had eaten lunch, she had been on his mind. There was no sight of her, so he went inside.

He closed the door and sniffed. Chocolate? He sniffed again. Why did he smell chocolate?

He went to the kitchen and looked around, but there was no food out at all. Certainly there was no chocolate cake. Had he been without real cooking for so long that he was beginning to hallucinate? Lucas had always been one to enjoy desserts if they were available, but he didn't crave sweets. Unable to explain the odd occurrence, he put it out of his mind.

With a flick of his wrist he tossed his empty drink can into the trash basket and went back to his office. The closed room no longer held any fears for him—his writer's block was a thing of the past. He sat down at the desk and began to type.

Several hours later he leaned back with a satisfied sigh. The chapter was finished and, as with the other one he had written, he sensed it was good. The story had unusual twists in it and was visual in its concept. It would make a terrific movie, if he did say so himself.

He closed the office door and went back into the main room. His letter to Aaron still lay where he had left it. Lucas had to chuckle. Now that he had calmed down from his first shock, he could see the humor in Jordan Lane's "kidnapping." His editor would be beside herself with the deadline looming so near, but she was a cold-hearted soul and not likely to worry about her writer as a person. Aaron was probably worried, but Lucas knew he, too, would find it amusing once he heard the whole story. Lucas wasn't concerned about his parents; they were on a cruise in the Mediterranean and wouldn't hear about it until they were home, after he had returned to Memphis.

Memphis. Lucas looked around his orderly cabin. There was no reason for him not to live here in the mountains. As long as he had a telephone and a post office, he didn't need much else. He could have an office in Rainie's house and use this place as a retreat the way he did now. The idea of riding a horse to work was rather appealing.

Did that mean he was going to propose? Lucas dropped onto the couch and stared at the cold ashes in the fireplace. Marriage was a serious business; he didn't want to rush into it. He loved Rainie, but surely it would be wiser to let time pass before he asked her for a permanent commitment.

He turned his eyes toward his office door. He certainly shouldn't propose to her until the book was finished. One of his iron-clad rules, following his experience trying to write during his divorce, was to do nothing to change his life or his environment while he was immersed in a book. A marriage proposal certainly fit the category of life changes.

Lucas leaned back and gazed up at the ceiling. Rainie had been good for him. Her fresh ideas and off-beat way of looking at things had been instrumental in breaking through his writer's block. She had given him far more to think about than all the reasons he couldn't force himself to get words on a page. He thought he might even use some of Rainie's qualities in his heroine. All his readers would love Rainie. So would his friends and family.

There was so much he wanted to show her. During his research trips, Lucas had discovered out-of-the-way inns and fascinating places all over the country. He had made friends from coast to coast in his search to make his novels as true to life as possible. Maybe Oscar or Billy could be hired to stay on the farm while he took Rainie around to show her his world. Lucas had to laugh. He was thinking like Jordan Lane!

Being a writer was basically lonely except for the research trips. Rainie would be a godsend at the end of the day. Her horses and the farm would give her plenty to do when he needed quiet for his work. The arrangement sounded perfect. Above all, he loved her, and he never wanted to be away from her again. As soon as the rough draft was finished, he would tell her so.

Lucas went to the table and picked up the letter. There must be a stamp somewhere. He rummaged through his office and the top drawer of the dresser in his bedroom. Finally he found one in the spare parts drawer in the kitchen. All the glue was rubbed off so he stuck it in place with rubber cement. He could mail it from Rainie's mail box and save himself a trip to town.

Whistling, he put the letter in the pocket of his jean jacket and went out to the barn to saddle the horse.

11

RAINIE STARED MOURNFULLY at the remains of the chocolate cake she had baked for Lucas. She had managed to stifle her tears, but four slices of the cake were gone, she was getting a stomachache, and she was no closer to solving her problem than she had been.

Was Lucas a kidnapper?

Once again she tried to reason away what seemed all too obvious. She had been in his cabin and in his barn and had seen no sign of Jordan Lane. Thus the letter had to be something other than the ransom note she had assumed it to be. She tried to recall exactly what it had said, but she had been so upset she could only recall parts of it. Jordan Lane was alive and well but hidden where no one could find him. This person, Aaron Tavish, would be contacted later. Who was Aaron Tavish? Rainie decided this must be Jordan Lane's editor. That would explain the Fifth Avenue address. Everyone knew editors lived in New York.

So where was Jordan Lane? A headache pounded behind her forehead. If Lucas *was* a kidnapper, wouldn't it follow that he was probably a liar? If someone kidnapped a famous writer and thought the victim could later identify his kidnapper, wouldn't it be smart to kill the victim? As no one would possibly want to pay a ransom for a dead body, wouldn't the kidnapper naturally say the victim was alive and well?

Rainie hated herself for thinking this thought. If her reasoning was correct, Lucas was a murderer as well as a kidnapper.

Suddenly there was a knock on the back door. Rainie jumped and was trembling as she went to answer it. "Who's there?"

"It's me," Lucas called out.

Her hands went clammy and her stomach flipped over. "Me, who?" she asked, stalling for time. Why had he come? Had he seen her leaving his cabin in the wrong direction and become suspicious?

"Lucas," he answered with a chuckle. "Open the door."

"I can't."

"Why not?"

She thought frantically. "I'm not dressed."

He laughed. "Good."

"Just a minute." She pressed her palms against her diaphragm and forced herself to draw a deep breath. She couldn't go to pieces, especially when she had no real proof Lucas was involved in any wrongdoing. Besides, she had seen enough movies and read enough books to know a person was usually safe until the villain realized he or she knew too much.

She opened the door wide enough to slip out, and closed it behind her. "Hi."

"You didn't have to dress on my account."

Rainie looked up at him and saw not a kidnapper but the man she loved. Instantly she felt disloyal for ever thinking ill of him, but she couldn't altogether dismiss her awful suspicions. "I didn't expect you."

"Okay if we go inside?"

"No!" The house seemed too private, too isolated if Lucas really was a kidnapper. "I mean, I have chores to do."

"I'll help you."

She had hoped he would leave and give her time to figure out what to do. "Help me?"

"Sure. What needs to be done first?"

She looked around for an answer. There really wasn't anything that couldn't wait until tomorrow when Billy and Oscar would be there, but she had to say something. Finally an idea came and her face brightened. "I need to put saddle soap on the bridles."

On the way to the barn, Rainie could feel his eyes boring into her back every step of the way. She was a painfully honest person, and she was extremely uncomfortable having to pretend nothing was wrong. Her first instinct was to come right out and ask him what the letter had meant, but that would necessitate her admitting she had not only gone into his house when he wasn't home, but that she had read his mail. If this was all an innocent misunderstanding, he might never forgive her deceitfulness. On the other hand, if he was a criminal, he might have to silence her for knowing too much. The best thing she could do was pretend she suspected nothing.

The tack room, located near the front of the barn, was as clean as any room in her house. From the cabinet containing jars of liniment, antiseptic, and the various other odds and ends she and the men used in tending to the animals, she got a jar of saddle soap and from the rag drawer beneath, two old socks.

The saddles were all mounted on padded wooden arms that were bolted to the wall. On another wall the bridles hung from pegs, each labeled with the name of the horse that was accustomed to that particular bit.

"Why are there more bridles than saddles?" Lucas asked as she handed him the one marked Blaze.

"The saddles are interchangeable, but I use a different bridle for each horse. When I sell a horse, the bridle goes with him. My grandmother taught me that. She was quite a horse trader. Although we didn't actually raise horses, we always kept a few to work Dad's cattle. I guess she sold the horses and bridles together because of her concern about passing germs to another animal or something. I never really heard the reason. Maybe it's because the horse gets used to the feel of one bridle and handles better that way. I guess wearing another horse's bridle would be similar to borrowing someone else's shoes." When she realized she was babbling, she made an effort to keep quiet. Lucas was looking at her strangely.

As they began working the cream into the leather, Rainie was disturbed by her thoughts.

"You're going to rub a hole in that spot," Lucas teased.

Rainie was immediately aware she'd been rubbing on January's bridle with unnecessary vigor, and determined she needed to pay closer attention to what she was doing, lest she give herself away.

"I thought saddle soap was used to soften stiff leather," he commented after a while. "This bridle is as pliable as it can be."

"Waterproofing," she said. "That's what we're doing—waterproofing."

"Is there something wrong?"

"Wrong? No. What could be wrong?" Her words came more rapidly than normal and her pitch was higher.

"I don't know. You've been acting strange ever since I got here."

"Nope, not me. Must be your imagination."

Lucas noticed she wasn't meeting his eyes, and she seemed pale.

"Are you feeling all right?"

"Perfectly fine. No, I've just got these chores to do. That's the thing about living on a ranch, there's always something that needs to be done."

He made no comment, but he knew she wasn't being straightforward with him. Maybe she had received bad news from home. "Have you heard from your parents lately?"

"Who? Oh, yes. We talk often. I've told them all about you." She looked at him as if she were gauging his reaction.

Lucas felt a twinge of guilt. She couldn't possibly have told them all about him, because she knew only part of the truth herself. He wished he could tell her who he really was, but the specter of writer's block was still too newly vanquished. He didn't want to do anything to staunch the flow of the story now that he was finally able to write again.

He stood and swapped Blaze's bridle for another one. Rainie was watching his every move, and when he turned and smiled at her, she ducked her head as if she hadn't been looking at him. "Are you upset about something?"

"Not me. What would I be upset about?"

Lucas stared at her with growing suspicion. Something was obviously bothering her, but she wasn't going to tell him what it was. He speculated that she might be linking him to that ridiculous news story about Jordan Lane being kidnapped, and a part of him hoped she was, so he would have a good reason to reveal his true identity. "Read any good books lately?" he asked, to give her an opening.

"No! I mean, I haven't had much time to read lately. Or to watch television or to listen to the radio. I've even considered canceling my newspaper subscription. I haven't read it in days. Weeks maybe."

Lucas frowned. "Is there something you're trying to tell me?"

"Not a thing."

"Is it something I've said? Something I didn't say?"

She jumped to her feet. "I have no idea what you're talking about. Look, let's leave this for Billy and Oscar and let's . . . clean up the loft."

"Clean up the loft?"

She hung January's bridle back on its hook and screwed the lid onto the saddle soap. "It's really a mess up there. If you'd rather go home, I understand."

"I'll help you."

Rainie's face clouded with misery. Why wouldn't he take the hint and leave?

She led the way to the narrow steps and looked up. This was as secluded as the house. Had she made a mistake? She felt him close behind her and hurried up the steps.

"What is there to do up here?" he asked as he looked around.

"All this loose hay needs to be tossed out. When we bale hay, we stack it up here, and this is all left over from bales that burst or what was dropped on the way to the hayricks. Here." She took one pitchfork and handed him the other one. "Toss it either into the ricks or out the end door and into the feed lot." She knew this was busy work, but Lucas might think this was necessary. She hoped the physical labor would prevent more conversation.

"I like the smell of hay," he said as he forked up a load of straw. "It reminds me of a simpler time."

"Oh?" She went to the far end of the loft and started to fork the hay out into the feed lot. Below her, the bedraggled horses looked up expectantly and ambled closer to feed.

"One of my grandfathers had cows, and when I was a boy I used to make forts in his hay bales. Those were happy times. I always made my sister be the cowboy and I was the Indian. She usually ended up tied to a stake."

"Do you see a lot of your sister now?"

"No. We've never been especially close."

"Does she live around here?"

"No."

She waited for him to elaborate, but as usual he seemed to think a short, uninformative answer was enough. "I got a letter from my brother Andy. He and his wife are expecting their first child in the autumn."

"That's nice."

"You like children?"

"Of course."

"But you don't have any."

"I also don't have a wife. Call me old-fashioned, but it seems I should have one of those before I have children." He grinned at her.

Rainie looked away. "I always thought I would have babies. I guess I'll get used to the idea of not raising a family eventually."

"It's still not too late."

She watched as his muscles flexed under his aqua polo sweater, and his biceps swelled as he tossed the hay through the square hole in the loft. She hadn't noticed him removing his jacket, but it lay on the hay behind him. With an effort she looked away. He might be heart-stoppingly handsome and she might love him, but what did she really know about him? Nothing. Nothing at all.

With increased vigor, she slipped the tines of her pitchfork under another pile of hay, and as she pitched it through the open doorway, a capricious breeze threw the dust back in her face.

Rainie shook her head and sputtered, spitting out the flecks of straw as she rubbed at her eyes. Suddenly she felt Lucas pull her hands away. "Don't do that," he said. "You might hurt yourself."

He took out his clean handkerchief and dusted the hay off her face. Rainie opened her eyes and met his. "Why are we doing this?" he asked.

"I told you. I need to clean out the loft so when we bale—"

"Rainie, nobody bales hay in the springtime."

As she cast about in her mind for a way to dispute this, Lucas took her pitchfork and tossed it onto the nearest bale of hay. "I think you had better tell me what's bothering you."

With a sigh, she raised her eyes to his. "I love you. I've tried all afternoon to fall out of love with you and I've failed."

"That's all it is?" He drew her into his arms and held her close. "I love you, too, and it scares me as much as it does you."

"It does?"

"I had no intention of ever loving anyone again. I wanted to keep my life simple and unfettered. Then you came along, and now I love you whether it's convenient or not. I guess these things never wait until the logical time rolls around. Love, babies and death, all seem to keep their own schedules."

She pressed her face against his chest and listened to the steady beat of his heart as she held tightly to his waist. "I don't know anything about you. Not really. How can I love you?"

He paused. "You may not know all the details of my life, but you know who I am. You said so yourself. It's almost as if our souls recognize each other, if you believe in such things." He sounded almost shy about admitting that he did.

"I think that's possible. Maybe even probable. I know I felt something for you right from the very first. Something I had never felt before."

"You've been good for me, Rainie. I can't tell you how much good you've done me already. Someday I'll tell you just how much."

She held him as his words soaked in. She had been a good influence. Did he mean that because of her, he saw his life of crime as deplorable? That due to her influence, he was willing to go straight? "Oh, Lucas," she murmured, "I hope I've been a very good influence on you. I can't think of anything that would please me more."

"You can't?" He sounded perplexed.

Rainie lifted her face to his and gazed deep into his brown eyes. "That was a beautiful thing for you to say."

He gave her a tender smile. "If I had known it was important to you, I'd have said so before now."

With a wavering smile, Rainie said, "Just remember you can confide in me anytime you feel like it."

He searched her face as if he wasn't too sure what she meant, but he said, "I love you. One of these days maybe I'll even learn to understand you." He glanced around at the loft. "Do we have to keep shoveling hay?"

"No," she replied with a laugh. "Not any more." Whatever mistakes he had made before he met her, he seemed to be willing to set straight. If she could keep him from a life of crime, anything she could do would be worth it. Whatever he had done, she loved him.

"Wait here."

She watched him go back to the steps and down to the barn below. He might have made mistakes, fallen in with the wrong people, been led astray, but with a good woman's love and encouragement, he could get back on the right path. She had been good for him; he had said so. Maybe through her love he could see that it was better to simply release Jordan Lane and forget about the ransom.

Or maybe he had unscrupulous friends and they were the real kidnappers. This made more sense, since he obviously wasn't holding a hostage at his cabin. Maybe Lucas was only the go-between. Rainie smiled with relief because this made perfect sense. It explained how someone as gentle as Lucas could be involved in such a crime and why there was no Jordan Lane to be found. The real kidnappers must have somehow convinced Lucas to act as the middle man and to type up the ransom letter and sign it with his name. Surely if Lucas wasn't actively involved in the kidnapping and was only the messenger, a judge would be lenient on him. Especially once her influence gave him a change of heart. Why, he might have already thrown the ransom letter away and be backing out of the scheme.

Lucas returned with a quilt from the tack room slung over his shoulder. He came to her and spread it over the billows of hay, then took both her hands in his and kissed each of her fingers. Cupping the base of her head in his palm, he drew her mouth up to meet his in a lingering, intensely sensual kiss. As they separated, he eased himself onto the pallet and drew her down beside him. "Hay looks soft, but it's like sitting on pliable needles. I thought this would make it much more comfortable for us."

She lay back and spread out her arms. "Perfect. It's like an old feather bed my grandmother had when I was little." Her lips felt swollen from the pressure of his passionate kiss, and she wet them with the tip of her tongue, wanting more.

He stretched out beside her, his head propped up on his hand. Leisurely he began unbuttoning her plaid shirt. "You look better in jeans than anyone I've ever seen," he said. "I can't get the picture out of my mind of you wearing these jeans and nothing else."

"I love your compliments. You make me feel so special."

"That's because you are."

"Not until you came along. I was just plain Rainie."

"Honey, you may have been a lot of things, but plain was never one of them."

"I like that. For you to call me honey."

"Some women would object."

"Not me. I know you mean it as an endearment."

Lucas removed her blouse, and when he unhooked and pulled away her bra, the cool spring air caused her rosy nipples to pout. Rainie let him gaze at her body in obvious admiration. "This is perfect attire for you."

"But not very practical for farm work," she teased. "Think of the sunburn I'd get. And Billy already embarrasses easily."

"I wouldn't want you like this in front of anyone but me." Lucas stroked his fingers over her breasts and her nipples beaded tighter. "You're so responsive to my touch."

"That's because my body is fond of yours." As he continued to caress her with his eyes, she pulled his sweater over his head. "Nice," she said as she stroked his smooth chest. "We wouldn't get much work done like this, but the view is great."

He swept his hand over her hips, cupping her jean's-clad bottom in his palm and pulling her close. When her breasts brushed his chest and mounded against him, Rainie caught her breath. It felt so good to have her bare skin pressed to his.

She laced her fingers through his hair and kissed him long and deep. Lucas held her close and returned her kiss with all the passion of a man in love. Placing a hand on either side of her head, he pulled back so he could study her eyes. His love was mirrored there for her to see, and for long moments they memorized the love each had for the other.

"You've made my life complete," he said at last. "I never knew what a void I had until you came along and filled it. I can't let you go."

"I'm not going anywhere."

Lucas was silent, and for a moment she thought he was about to confess the error he had made in befriending the kidnappers. "No," he said at last, "we mustn't leave each other. Somehow we can work it out."

He laid her back on the soft cotton quilt and unfastened her jeans. Tenderly he rubbed her smooth stomach, dipping a finger into the depression of her navel and then caressing upward to again capture her breast.

Lowering his head, he drew her nipple into his mouth and sucked gently. Rainie moaned with pleasure, the sound as soft as mist. With knowing strokes, Lucas ran his tongue over the tightening bud and teased it to throbbing eagerness. Rainie guided his head to her other breast and let her head rock back as she gave herself over to his pleasure.

When he pulled her jeans lower on her hips, Rainie lifted herself, and as she helped him pull them off, she kicked away her shoes. He smiled down at her. "I never knew farm girls wore such lacy underwear."

"You've never heard of the farmer's daughter?" she asked with a laugh.

Lucas slipped his fingers under the lace band of her panties and ran the back of his fingers over her skin. "You feel so good. Like satin, but warm."

His fingers grew bolder, and Rainie moved her hips forward against his hand. "I want you," she whispered. "Whenever I'm near you, I always want you. No matter how many times you satisfy me, I always want you again."

"You're in love. I feel the same way about you."

Together they unfastened his jeans, and he removed them for her. The sunlight through the open door warmed their bodies, and dust motes from the hay floated like shimmering gold in the still air. "I want to remember this forever," she whispered. "You beside me on this quilt, the way the sunlight falls on you, the smell of the hay, everything."

"We'll remember it," he replied. "This is one of those perfect times that will stay with us forever."

"I like to think of us like that—as a couple. As two halves that make up a whole."

"Rainie—"

She put her fingertips to his lips. "I'm not asking for a commitment or for you to promise anything at all. I only wanted to tell you how I feel."

"I wish it were all as simple as it ought to be. I wish I could give you all the promises you want to hear. In time—"

"Hush," she whispered. "I only want you to love me."

Lucas drew off her panties and pulled her close for his kiss, their bodies fitting together. He rolled with her so that she tumbled over him and lay on her side, their lips still pressed together in a passionate kiss. She felt his questing hand as he stroked her and explored the mysteries of her body. Rainie murmured and shifted to give him easier access to her.

With consummate skill, Lucas loved her, and Rainie felt as if she floated to the music he was playing on her soul. Higher and higher he brought her, strumming her nerves with his touch and singing the melody of love with his kisses.

As she reached her peak he entered her, and the sensation of him deep within her triggered waves of passion. Rainie pushed against him, drawing him even deeper, and the ecstasy exploded within her.

When the pulsing sensations began to abate, Lucas moved deep inside her, urging her to climb the heights again. Rainie's body responded eagerly.

This time when she felt him holding back to let her enjoy her satisfaction, she moved against him more insistently, and he cried out as his body answered hers. Tightly they held to each other as their passions were satisfied.

Rainie lay contentedly in his arms, hoping the moment would last forever. Her muscles were in a state of deep relaxation and her thoughts were misty and of no more substance than dreams. She loved him and for the moment that was enough. There was no future, no past, and certainly no problems. "Life feels easy when you're in love," she observed.

Lucas stroked his hand over her hip but didn't answer.

"I wonder if anyone else in the world is as happy as I am right this minute."

"I'm glad I make you happy," he said.

"Happy and confused and excited and satisfied. My emotions are on a roller coaster with you."

"I know the feeling. When I arrived, I thought you were mad at me, and I couldn't figure out what I had done."

She paused. "I wasn't mad. Just worried . . . and a little scared."

He hugged her close. "Sometimes I feel that way, too, but it's not for much longer."

"It isn't?"

He lifted her chin so that she gazed into his eyes. He had considered telling her his true identity now that his writer's block was no longer a problem, but he knew she was too curious and impetuous to be able to leave him alone so he could get his novel quickly written. After all, he was her favorite author, and he was sure she would want to watch him work and would have hundreds of questions. "I can't explain, but something is going on that I can't tell you about. However, it will be over soon, and after that I'll be free to make all the commitments you could ever want to hear."

"You will?" Her eyes grew wide and troubled. "When will it be over?"

"I'm not sure, but the way things have been going, I'd say within a few weeks."

"The way things are going?"

He kissed her lightly. "I can't explain now so please don't ask me. As soon as I can, I'll tell you everything."

"You . . . aren't in any kind of trouble, are you?"

With a laugh, he said, "Not any more, thanks to you. As soon as I'm free to talk about it, I'll tell you what a good influence you've been on me."

"A few weeks?" she repeated. "Couldn't you do whatever it is you have to do sooner than that?"

"Maybe. But for me to do that, I'll have to be away from you."

Her eyes searched his.

"I don't want to be away from you, Rainie. I want to be right by your side every day for the rest of my life. No," he said as she opened her mouth to speak. "No questions."

"Does it have anything to do with—"

"That's a question," he interrupted. "I've already told you more than I should have."

She reached up and touched his dark beard. "What do you look like without this?" Maybe if he shaved it, she thought, they could hide out in Mexico until the statute of limitations was up. How long would that be on a kidnapping charge?

He gave her a questioning look. "One day soon I'll show you."

"Have you ever considered moving to Mexico?"

"Mexico?" he asked in confusion. "No. Have you?"

"Not really, but I would if you wanted to. Or if you ever . . . felt the need to. I speak Spanish."

"That's nice, Rainie, but you're doing another tap dance on my mind. I don't quite follow your train of thought."

She smiled. "As long as you love me, is it necessary?"

"It must not be because you often lose me, and I still love you."

"I love you, too, Lucas. And remember, no matter what happens, I'll always love you. Any . . . mistakes . . . you've made in the past, I can forgive."

"Well, there have been other women, but . . ."

"I'm not talking about that. And I'm not asking questions. I just wanted you to know that . . . I forgive you."

"Thank you," he said without any comprehension.

"Can you spend the night? I'll pull out all the stops and make chili cheeseburgers."

"How lucky I am to find a gourmet cook right here in Lupine," he said with a laugh.

"Don't knock it until you've tried it. My chili cheeseburgers are famous with all my friends."

"I'll have to take a rain check. I really need to get my business finished just as quickly as I can, and in order to do that, I'll have to put a lot of effort into it. I don't know what snags, if any, I may run into, but I'm afraid I may run out of time. It will be better for both of us in the long run if I get back to what I must do and get through with it."

"Run out of time? Business? Does this mean I won't be seeing you until you finish?" The laughter left her eyes.

"Sweetheart, don't look so crestfallen. I'll be back down the mountain before you know it." He paused and pressed his forehead to hers so that their noses touched. "That's not really true. I'm going to miss you like hell every minute we're apart."

"I already miss you," she sighed.

Lucas hugged her again, then rolled to his feet. Rainie watched as he collected his clothes, then she also got up.

They dressed in silence as if words would make their temporary parting too real. When she was clothed again, Rainie picked up the quilt and neatly folded it. "I'll keep this up here," she said. "For when you return." She looked at him through the slanting rays of late sunlight. "You really will be back, won't you? Nothing can go wrong?"

"Of course not."

"And what you're about to do has something to do with me being a good influence? Can you tell me that much?"

"Yes. Now no more questions. I've already said too much."

"I understand," she said faintly. He must be about to break away from the kidnappers, and she wondered if that was as dangerous as it sounded. "Lucas, take care of yourself."

He grinned at her. "I always do."

Almost ceremoniously, she laid the quilt on a back bale of hay. She stroked the quilt's bright, double-ring pattern. A lot might happen before she saw him again. He might get in as much trouble from the kidnappers as he was in with the law. She wondered how such a sensitive, intelligent man as Lucas could have become embroiled in this nightmare. One thing must have led to another, and he became tangled in the web before he realized what was happening. Nothing else made sense. If he was caught, he would probably go to prison for his involvement, however unintentional it may have been. A shudder went through her at the thought that they might be separated for years while he served his time. And she had heard that prison changed men, and never for the better. Would he still love her? Would she still love him?

"I know all this sounds secretive and odd," he said, "but you have to trust me. I'll explain everything as soon as I can."

She forced a smile and nodded. "I'll wait for you. Forever if need be."

"I'm only asking for a few weeks. It will be hard, but it will be better this way."

He picked up his jean jacket and slung it casually over his shoulder. With his arm around Rainie, he guided her toward the steps.

As he saddled Red, she watched with a heavy heart. She felt like a Colonial woman seeing her lover off to war. Whatever Lucas was riding into might be every bit as dangerous.

Lucas finished tightening the cinch and dropped the stirrup back into place. He turned to her as if he were reluctant to leave. "I guess this is it."

She nodded, unable to take her eyes from him. She couldn't think about him going to prison. He might not even get caught if he was trying to get out of the mess he was in. But it was possible that if something went wrong, she might not ever see him again. Rainie wanted Lucas back safe and sound. Dead heroes made poor lovers. She hoped she wasn't going to cry.

"Cheer up, honey," he encouraged. "It's only for a few days. But promise me you won't come up to see me. It's important."

Rainie wondered how she could promise and still leave a loophole.

"I mean it. You can't come to the cabin. Promise."

Reluctantly she nodded. "I promise. I won't come to the cabin until you ride down and tell me it's all right."

"Or to the barn or meadow," he persevered.

"Okay, okay. I promise."

He nodded in satisfaction. "I'm sorry to be that way, but for me to finish what I have to do in the quickest possible time, I have to have no interruptions." He drew her close for a final kiss, then gazed deep into her eyes. "I'm going to miss you, Rainie."

"I'll miss you, too." The words seemed so bland compared to the worry and fear she felt. For Lucas's sake she had to be strong, so she smiled.

He turned to mount, then stopped. Reaching into his jacket pocket, he pulled out a white envelope. "I almost forgot. Will you mail this for me?"

Rainie saw "Aaron Tavish, 300 Fifth Avenue" staring up at her, and she froze.

"Is something wrong?"

"No! No, nothing's wrong." She took the envelope from him as if it contained snakes.

"Don't forget to mail it. This is very important. Rainie, did you hear me?"

"Yes!" She held it gingerly as she stared at the address. "I hear you."

"I'll explain about this letter when I tell you about all the rest of it. Okay?"

"Dandy."

Lucas swung up into the saddle and winked at her. "I love you."

"I love you, too."

He nudged Red into a trot that carried him out of the barn, then let the horse break into a canter as he rode toward the orchard.

"Be careful!" she called after him. He lifted his hand in a wave.

Rainie was left alone with the damning letter. Once more she read the address. There was no return address, but that was hardly surprising under the circumstances. How could Lucas break off with the kidnappers if he was still mailing their ransom letter?

She glanced up to get a last look at Lucas as he disappeared into the woods that bordered the old wagon road. Did this mean he hadn't changed his mind about being involved? She had no way of knowing.

Filled with anguish, she stared down at the letter. She could think of nothing she could do that would help Lucas extricate himself from those criminals—he would have to manage on his own. She felt terribly frustrated and enraged that these people, whoever they were, had taken advantage of Lucas and were using him in this way. Rainie looked again at the letter she was holding, and suddenly realized they were getting her involved, as well! This, however, she *could* do something about.

Resolutely she went to the old oil drum where she deposited her trash for burning, and tossed the letter onto a pile of last week's junk mail, food boxes and feed bags.

12

AFTER TURNING RED LOOSE in his pen, Lucas gave him a measure of feed and took his saddle and bridle into the storeroom. By comparison with Rainie's well-organized tack room, this one came up pretty short, but soon Lucas hoped not to be using it at all. If everything went as he hoped, he would be living in Rainie's cozy house and using this cabin only for retreats. He lifted the saddle well off the floor and looped the noose in the hay rope around the saddle horn. He hung the bridle over the horn and laid the saddle blanket, hairy side up, over the saddle seat.

By now the sun had sunk low behind the mountain, casting long purple shadows from the trees across the meadow. Lucas paused on his way to the cabin and surveyed the scene. In order to finish the rough draft in two weeks, he was going to have to spend every available minute at the typewriter. The hardest chapters were done. Motivation was established and his characters had come to life for him. All he had to do now was let the details of the story unfold. He knew from past experience that the next few days would be gruelling, but working this way had its rewards in that he often had to do fewer revisions because his concentration wasn't interrupted. And writing the rough draft was the part of writing he liked best. As the story revealed itself, he would record it, taking breaks only for the necessities of life and as little sleep as was humanly possible. He was eager to begin.

After lighting the lamps against the gathering darkness, he opened a big can of beef stew and put it on to simmer. Later, when hunger hit him, he would eat; otherwise, he would be a slave to the typewriter.

With a flourish, Lucas opened the office door. His desk was there, filling almost every corner. Research books he had brought with him from Memphis were piled high on a wooden bookcase. From his lower left desk drawer, he got a ream of paper. He surveyed his tools of the trade like a warrior sizing up his armaments for battle, and he smiled. This book was good, and it was destined to become his first feature-length movie. Lucas pulled out the chair and sat down, his fingers poised over the keys as he composed his thoughts. The story of the pioneer families sprang into his mind and began to tell itself. Lucas started typing.

RAINIE TOSSED all night, worrying about Lucas. Was he so foolhardy as to confront the kidnappers openly, or would he find a way to ease out of the gang without notice? Lucas seemed to be the straightforward type, and this worried Rainie to distraction.

Finally, as the sky paled toward dawn, she fell into an exhausted sleep filled with nightmares. When she awoke, the sun was well into the sky, and she could hear Billy calling to Oscar as they went about their work.

She sat up and rubbed her aching shoulders, thinking she would have felt better if she had stayed up all night. Quickly she dressed and made up her bed, then she went into the kitchen for a cup of coffee.

She couldn't bear the idea of Lucas being involved with criminals. What if they hurt him? Naturally she was concerned about Jordan Lane, too, but she was in love with Lucas.

As she sat at the table trying to guess what might be happening up the mountain, a dozen scenarios presented themselves, each more horrible than the one before. The only thing keeping her sane was the knowledge that Lucas seemed confident about handling it. He seemed to have a plan he was sure would succeed.

A nagging foreboding began to dawn on her. Lucas knew how to handle it. He knew exactly what to do to safely disentangle himself.

And he had told Rainie to mail the letter to Aaron Tavish. And she had thrown it away!

Rainie slammed her coffee cup down on the table, sloshing coffee over the rim, and hurried outside. Oscar had set up his blacksmith's tripod and was trimming January's hooves. Blaze and another yearling waited nearby, looking on with resignation. Rainie waved a distracted greeting to him and circled the barn to the area where she burned her trash. As she rounded the last corner, she was greeted with thick, black smoke roiling upward from the barrels, and she heard the loud cracks and pops of burning debris.

Billy turned to her with a grin. "You slept late, Boss Lady. We were beginning to think you'd taken up the night life."

"What are you doing!" she gasped.

"Burning trash. It was starting to stack up. I should have done this last week, but I didn't get around to it."

"You're burning trash!"

"Rainie, are you okay? This is supposed to be part of my job. You told me so." His concern was evident in his face.

"Have you burned all of it? Every bit?"

"Well, sure. I just throw it all in the barrel and set fire to it. It's burned down to the last dregs now. Why?"

"Nothing." Rainie felt stiff inside.

"Did I do something wrong?"

She shook her head. "No, Billy, you did right. I'm the one who made a mistake." And it was a big one, she thought. Thanks to her thoughtless action, the ransom note was gone forever!

She trod on heavy feet back to the house, puzzling over what the consequences to her blunder might be. Maybe Lucas was timing his departure to Tavish's receipt of that letter. Maybe when it never arrived, the gang would see they couldn't trust Lucas. Lucas, or Jordan Lane, or both might be shot!

From the hall closet where she kept things she rarely used, such as boxes of Christmas decorations and various craft supplies she meant to use someday, she pulled out a battered carrying case. It was her old typewriter, a so-called portable that had seen her through high school and college.

She maneuvered the heavy, cumbersome box onto the top of the kitchen table and unlatched the hooks that held the cover in place. She seldom used it. The last person to borrow it had been Tom Hanford, who had needed it to type up some handouts for his last campaign. The "h" key hadn't worked right since.

She had no time to worry about that. Rainie found some sheets of typing paper and rolled one into the machine. Her hands felt cold as she held them poised over the keys. What had the letter said?

Closing her eyes, she struggled to remember. "Dear Aaron," she wrote, then frowned. Nobody would send a ransom letter that started off "Dear."

She pulled the paper out and crumpled it into the wastebasket. Rolling in another sheet, she typed, "Aaron."

Skipping down two spaces as she had been taught in typing class, she paused again to think. "I have Jordan Lane, and he is alive and well. He is hidden in the mountains where you will never find him."

Rainie stopped. This was harder than she had expected. She had thought the words on the ransom letter would stay with her forever. What else had it said? "Quit looking for him. I will contact you soon about the ransom."

Another Rainbow

She sat back and read through her letter twice. There might be a word wrong here or there, but this was pretty close. She was going to do one thing different, however. Lucas had foolishly signed his name, even though it had only been his first, but she wasn't about to repeat his mistake and give the authorities proof positive he was involved.

Nervously she rummaged through the antique secretary where she kept her bill-paying supplies until she found a business-length envelope. Carefully she folded the letter into it, but before sealing the envelope, her fingers faltered. Could fingerprints be lifted from paper? She didn't know, but just to be sure, she took the letter back out and rubbed it with a dishtowel. Then she restuffed the envelope, licked the flap, and sealed it.

She rolled the envelope into the typewriter and correctly typed "Aaron Tavish." But she started the second line with 500, which was wrong. She started to cross it out with X's, but decided this was too important. After a diligent search, she found her bottle of typing correction fluid and dabbed a small amount of it over the 5. Leaning forward, she blew on it until it dried, then typed "300 Fifth Avenue, New York, New York," and paused. What was the zip code? She couldn't remember.

Rainie went to the phone and dialed the post office. "Ed? This is Rainie. I'm fine. How's Myrtle? Good. Listen, can you give me the zip code for New York City? The street address? That's right, there would be a lot of zip codes for a city that size." She deliberated giving him the address for a minute, but concluded she would have to tell him if she wanted the right zip. When he responded, she said, "That's it! Yes, I'm sure of it. Thanks a lot, Ed. Tell Myrtle I said hello."

She hung up and typed in the zip code.

Holding the envelope in both hands, Rainie studied it. The address was right. She was positive of that. If it wasn't for the way the H dropped half a space below the other characters, this envelope would look exactly like the one she had thrown away.

Was she doing the right thing? Rainie wished she knew. Somehow it didn't seem right to type up a ransom note and send it, but she was afraid to do anything else. Lucas's life, as well as that of Jordan Lane's, might rest upon this letter being received by Aaron Tavish.

Rainie was still searching for a stamp when she saw the mailman's battered Toyota coming down the road. She ran out into the front yard, waving her arms and calling for him to stop. Her dogs, thinking this was a game, ran with her.

The mail carrier waved back and pulled over to her mailbox. He sat in the middle of the front seat, his left foot in position to work the brakes and gas pedal, his right hand in reach of the mailbox.

"Thanks for stopping, Jack. Do you have a stamp I can buy? I'm out and I have to get this in the mail."

"Sure thing." Jack reached into the glove compartment and sorted through a mound of rubber bands, finally unearthing a roll of stamps. "Will just one do it?"

"It's not heavy." She handed the letter into the car as Jack tore off a stamp, licked it and put it in place.

"New York City," he mused. "You know, I don't reckon I ever carried a letter addressed to New York. Seen some going to Washington, D.C. And one year we had a feller what wrote to somebody in Canada. His sister, I think she was. But he died."

"That's too bad." Rainie wished Jack wasn't showing so much interest in the letter he still held in his hands.

"He was old. Come out here to retire. Never did fit in. Back in '53, that was."

"Nineteen fifty-three? You remember mail from that far back?"

"Yep." Jack grinned with pride and scratched his thin white hair. "Don't much get by me." He dropped the letter into a smaller bag. "I'll send it off as soon as I get back to the post office, or Ed will, one or the other. Have a good day now."

"Thanks," she said faintly. "I'll try." She wanted suddenly to grab the letter out of the mailbag and run to tell Lucas she knew all about everything. But that could endanger the man she loved. Besides, Jack was already driving away with the letter in the control of the United States government.

Praying she had done the right thing, Rainie went back to the house.

AARON TAVISH nodded as his assistant brought in the day's mail. Ever since Lucas had gone missing, Aaron had been a bundle of nerves. He balanced the phone between his ear and shoulder and made noncommittal responses to the party on the other end. Over the wire buzzed the angry voice of one of his clients with complaints about her editor at a well-known publishing house. Aaron was accustomed to such calls from this particular client since the woman had a reputation for being hard to get along with, even when working with the most tactful of editors, as this one was.

As the writer launched into her third repetition of the editor's faults, he began shuffling through his mail. Most were large, brown mailing envelopes which likely contained novel synopses and chapters. One larger box obviously contained a manuscript. He glanced at the return address and nodded in satisfaction. This was a completed manuscript from one of his clients, and a quick check of the file on his desk verified the book was in early. The smaller envelopes usually contained either query letters or routine correspondence from his clients, and on occasion, a bill or two. As he sifted through them, one plain white business envelope caught his eye. It had no return address, and the "h"s dropped half a space below the line. Obviously this had come from the desk of an un-published author who couldn't even be bothered to use a good typewriter. By the weight, he knew there would be no stamped, self-addressed envelope enclosed as was the custom. He tapped it lightly on the desk as he agreed with the caller that the editor should be boiled in oil, then tried to suggest that some of the editor's revision points might be valid. The writer cut him off with another tirade.

Aaron opened his lap drawer and fished out a roll of ant-acid mints, hoping to stave off the return of his ulcer. He popped a couple of tablets in his mouth and jotted a note on his deskpad to buy more.

While the writer droned on, Aaron looked back at the envelope. He was tempted to save a step and toss it unopened into the wastebasket, but professionalism prevailed. Maybe there would be a miracle, and it would be a query from a literary genius who couldn't afford a good typewriter.

He picked up a teak and silver letter opener sent to him by a happier client, and slit open the top of the envelope. Inside was a single sheet of paper.

Aaron,
I have Jordan Lane, and he is alive and well. He is hidden in the mountains where you will never find him. Quit looking for him. I will contact you soon about the ransom.

An expletive was out of his mouth before Aaron could stop it, and the phone fell from his shoulder, clattering onto the floor. "Hello! Hello!" he shouted as he grabbed up the receiver. "I have to call you back!" He slammed the phone down and snatched up the paper again. "Holy..."

Again he scanned the brief message. With a trembling hand, he dialed the police.

Within minutes he was connected with the FBI agent who was handling the Jordan Lane kidnapping case. "Leo Bratcher here."

"This is Aaron Tavish. In New York. I'm Jordan Lane's agent."

"Yes, Mr. Tavish?" Bratcher sounded bored, as if he, too, were reading through his mail as they talked.

"I have it! I have the ransom letter!"

At once Bratcher's voice became steely. "Ransom letter?"

"I'll read it to you." When he finished, he said, "It came in today's mail."

"Why would it come to you? Why not to his parents?"

"How should I know?"

"You say there's no signature or return address?"

Tavish frowned. "You think perhaps this kidnapper is stupid? With a name and address we could look him up in the phone book."

Bratcher seemed to be thinking about that. "It would seem to be someone who knows a lot about Lane, or Dalton, whichever way you know him."

"What do you mean?"

"How many people know a writer's agent? You'd expect the letter to come to his parents or to his publishing house."

Tavish swallowed. "This may be proof they have him. Lucas would have them contact me."

"I see." Again there was a pause, as if the man were digesting this. "What's the postmark say?"

Tavish reached for the envelope and had to squint to make out the blurred letters. "Lupine, Tennessee."

"Lupine. Never heard of it."

"I think Lucas has a summer place near there. He mentioned it once."

Bratcher grunted. "I have to ask you this, Mr. Tavish. Do you think Lane is staging all this?"

"Dalton. His name is Lucas Dalton! No, I don't think he's staging this." Tavish's temper flared at the idea.

"Why not? You say the letter was mailed from the vicinity of his summer house."

"I know Lucas, and he would never do such a thing."

"From what I hear, Jordan Lane is capable of any stunt."

"Jordan Lane doesn't exist. He's only a pseudonym. All his exploits are dreamed up by a publicity agent."

Again Bratcher grunted an acknowledgment. "Still, it seems funny."

"Not to me! Lucas is my friend as well as my client!"

"I naturally didn't mean funny in the comic sense."

"Listen to the way the words are written. 'He is,' 'you will,' 'I will.' Not a contraction in the lot. His publicist always uses contractions. Drives us crazy. And one of the keys is bent. See, the 'h' drops below the line. Where would Lucas get a typewriter like that?"

"I see. Look, Mr. Tavish, I'm going to send a man over to get that letter. It's obviously important evidence, so don't lose it."

"As if I could lose it!" Aaron Tavish gripped the receiver tightly. "Tell him to hurry. Lucas is in danger."

"Yes, sir. We've assumed that from the beginning."

Tavish hung up. Almost at once his phone rang again. It would be a client or an editor. On the third ring, his answering machine took the call.

Whoever wrote this letter had Lucas; Tavish didn't doubt that for a minute. Although it wasn't confidential that he was Jordan Lane's agent, it certainly wasn't widely known outside the publishing industry. He hoped and prayed that Lucas hadn't been harmed. Tavish had handled enough nonfiction to know that hostages didn't always fare well. He reached for the roll of antacid tablets.

LUCAS GROANED and shifted in his chair. All his muscles ached, and when he stretched, his back and shoulders audibly popped. He ran his fingers through his tousled hair and over his beard. Both needed a trim. He looked into his mug and found it was empty, though he didn't remember drinking the coffee.

As he got to his feet he noticed his legs felt rubbery from having been in one position for so long, and the stack of typed pages next to his typewriter was further proof of how long he had been there. Halfway. He was halfway through the rough draft.

Deciding it was time for another break, he ambled into the kitchen, and as he waited for more coffee to brew, he looked at the calendar. Was this Wednesday? Sleeping at odd times, he was losing track of the days. Not that it mattered. Until the rough draft was complete, all his days and nights were the same.

He took a bite out of a doughnut from the box in the pantry and noticed it had gone stale. There was plenty of canned food to fall back on, but most of it needed to be heated to taste palatable. Cooking and washing dishes took too much time. He opened a can of pork and beans and stuck a spoon in it.

When the coffee was ready, he poured himself a cup, then looped several doughnuts over the handle of the spoon. Lunch in hand, Lucas went back into the office.

For the next half hour he typed and ate alternately. The story was forming clear and unbroken in his mind. Occasionally he glanced at the outline to be sure he was still on the right track. Using a typewriter when he was accustomed to a word processor had taken some getting used to, but he was making good progress.

The next time he looked up, the living room was dark. Lucas got up and threw away the can that had contained his lunch and rinsed the spoon. Getting his flashlight off the table by the door, he went outside and across the meadow to the barn. Red whickered expectantly.

"Hungry?" Lucas asked as he scooped a coffee can in the bag of horse feed. "I'll bet you miss Rainie's horses. I know for sure I miss Rainie." He poured the feed into the square trough and patted the horse's neck. "Hang in there, old fellow. Just a few days more and we can rejoin the living."

He watched as Red ate the feed, kernels of corn and oats dripping from his lips. The horse rippled the skin on his back and swished his tail. Far away a night bird called.

Lucas's eyes grew thoughtful. Indians would make such a sound as they circled a cabin for attack. Again the note came through the air, and Lucas pursed his lips to repeat it. One note, not two separate ones, and it curved down, not up. He looked back at Red. Horses picked up grain with their lips, not teeth. These were details that would add dimension to his story.

Lucas patted Red again. "Thanks, pal. You've been a big help." Quickly he struck out in the dark toward the glowing windows of his cabin. As he went, he practiced the call of the night bird.

RAINIE SAT in her dark bedroom, gazing up at the mountain that loomed black against the starry sky. Somewhere in the gloom, Lucas was probably sleeping. Were the kidnappers at his cabin? Was Jordan Lane there? If only there was some way she could help!

Restlessly she went to the living room and turned on a lamp. From the bookshelves next to her fireplace, she selected one of Jordan Lane's earlier books and curled up on the couch. She had read this book twice before, so she paid little attention to the dust jacket and didn't notice Lucas's eyes smiling at her from the younger, clean-shaven photo on the back. Reading the book made Rainie feel closer to Lucas for some reason. Probably, she assumed, because of the link he had with Jordan Lane. Maybe he was biding his time in order to help the author escape.

Rainie drew the hem of her nightgown over her bare toes and continued reading. A deep regret filled her that an author of such talent was in danger. Naturally she would never know Jordan Lane—she probably would never even get a glimpse of him—but she felt as if she knew him through his work. She wondered if he was anything like the heroes he portrayed. His characters seemed unlike the stories she had read about Jordan Lane's private life—if the life of anyone who lived in such glamor and high style could be considered private. She hoped he would come away from his ordeal unharmed.

She prayed Lucas would, too.

13

LUCAS SAT BACK and grinned. With great deliberation, using all capital letters, he typed THE END. He knew his editor, who would be working on the manuscript in the weeks and months to come, would delete those two words before it was typeset, but he needed to see them in print. He ached from head to toe, and his eyes were burning with fatigue. But the rough draft was finished. He stood and flexed his legs, then his back and arms. After pulling the page from the typewriter, he placed it facedown on the stack with the others. Only a few sheets remained of the ream of paper he had started with. He had cut it close on this one. Having to drive into town after more paper would have been a terrible distraction.

Almost ceremoniously, Lucas turned over the pile of paper, straightened it, and banded it with a couple of rubber bands before stuffing it into a padded mailing envelope, which he had already addressed to his agent during one of those awful days he'd had writer's block. Once he got a copy made, he would substitute the copy for the original in the envelope and and send it on its way. On one of the remaining sheets of typing paper, he scribbled a note to Aaron Tavish— he couldn't face typing another word.

Here it is, and you'll notice it's on time. Even allowing for slow mail delivery, you can get this draft to my editor before it's due. This is a first cut, but I think you'll agree it won't need much revision. I found a great way to break writer's block—wait until you meet her. Now I'm going to sleep, bathe and propose. I'll explain everything later

—Lucas

He slipped the letter in with the manuscript and set the package aside. The note probably didn't make much sense, but by the time it got to Aaron, he would most likely already have contacted him by phone.

One by one, Lucas blew out the lamps and darkness slowly followed his path. When he reached his bedroom, he paused only long enough to step out of his shoes and shuck off his clothes. He lay down with a groan and stretched out his aching limbs on the cool sheets. Nothing quite described the way he always felt upon finishing a book. It resembled the afterglow of lovemaking.

Rainie. All at once he missed her with a longing that shook him to the depths. While he was on his marathon of composition he hadn't allowed himself to think of her. Now nothing stood in their way.

He buried his head in the soft pillow and pictured her there beside him. If he had Rainie around, he would have to learn a new way of turning out a rough draft. That might be a good idea. Other writers didn't force themselves into a writing frenzy, and he would be willing to bet they weren't this drained and exhausted when they finished a novel. If he had Rainie in his bed and at his table he was sure he could learn new methods of creating.

As he willed his tense muscles to relax, he thought of the times he had spent with Rainie—of her laughing over her shoulder as they rode horseback, of her eating canned stew and liking it, of her naked body shimmering like a pearl in the slanting golden rays of her hayloft. He had known for a long time that his method of writing wasn't good for him, and with Rainie's help he would change it. She had been good for him, and the thought of her filled him with love.

How would he propose? It had to be just right because she would remember it forever. Women liked to have such memories to look back on. As a writer he should be able to come up with a romantic proposal that would give her a shining memory that would last well into her old age.

He fell asleep thinking of phrases to use when he asked her to share his life.

TOM HANFORD was sweeping out the four cells that comprised Lupine's jail. They were rarely used, except for an occasional drunk who needed to sleep off a binge or a hothead who was determined to fight but who had no real meanness in him. The county jail housed the convicted criminals. When the outer office door opened and shut, Tom called out, "That you, Eva Jean?"

"Sheriff Hanford?" a man's voice called.

Tom leaned the broom against the wall and went into the office. "I'm Sheriff Hanford. What can I do for you?"

"Leo Bratcher. I'm with the FBI."

"The FBI?" Tom repeated.

"I'm following a lead on the Jordan Lane case. I guess you've heard of it."

"Well, sure. I'm the one that sent word about there being a stranger over in Roan Oak. But that was a couple of weeks ago. Good thing it wasn't a house on fire or it would have burned down by the time you got here."

Bratcher and the two men with him didn't smile. "Arson is involved?" Bratcher asked.

"Never mind. Have a seat." Tom sat on his scarred chair and leaned his forearms on the desk. The three men in dark suits continued to stand. After a moment Tom got to his feet. He knew he was being snubbed, and he didn't like it. Manners were cheap to come by. "You boys have any credentials?" he asked.

Bratcher reached in his coat pocket and drew out his identification. The other two followed his lead. Tom read enough to nod grudgingly. "You're federal boys all right. Any particular reason why you're here in Lupine instead of talking to Sheriff Odom over in Roan Oak?" He put a deliberate drawl in his voice to intentionally irritate the one called Bratcher.

"I'll come right to the point." From his other pocket, Bratcher withdrew a photocopy of a letter and a postmarked envelope. "As you can see, the postmark means this letter was mailed from Lupine, not Roan Oak. We think the kidnappers may be hiding out here, and buying groceries in Roan Oak to throw off suspicion."

"Could be the other way around, too. Neither one makes any sense. A stranger around here would stand out like a sore thumb."

"Look at this letter and tell us if you know anything about it."

Tom took the photocopy and glanced at it. He was about to say one unsigned typed letter looked pretty much like any other one, when he noticed the way the "h"s dropped below the line. With a scowl, he scrutinized it more closely.

"Does it mean anything to you?"

"Looks to me like somebody or other is holding Jordan Lane around here. Isn't that what it means to you?" He was trying to remember where he had seen type like that before.

Bratcher impatiently sighed. "Obviously. Something about that letter caught your attention, in particular. Didn't it?"

"Nope. But maybe if I look again." Tom sat back down and perused the letter while fingering the stubble on his chin. As if he were looking for something else, he pulled out the lower drawer of his desk where he kept his campaign literature. The type with the dropped "h" leaped up at him.

"Are there any abandoned cabins around here where a hideout could be established?"

Tom shut the drawer. "I reckon there are dozens. As thick as these woods are, there could be people living up there that don't know electricity has been invented."

"You aren't being much help." Bratcher glared at him suspiciously. His two silent companions followed suit.

"Look, there's not much I can do to help you. Once in a while during deer season, I come across a cabin that I never knew was there. And I've lived here all my life. Some of these places don't even have tracks leading to them. A lot of the folks that live in the mountains don't ever have cars, and those that do park them near the road and walk through the woods to their homes. Lupine isn't like a city where every house has an address and power lines going to it."

He looked back at the letter, then handed it to Bratcher. "Now if it was me, I'd go over to Roan Oak and talk to Sheriff Joe Odom or I'd go to the post office and ask Ed or Jack if they recall handling this envelope. I can't help you."

Bratcher took the paper back and nodded, his cold eyes saying he hoped Tom wasn't playing games with him. He left and his two partners fell into step behind him.

Tom was grimacing as he pulled out the lower drawer again. He knew whose typewriter had an "h" like that. He had broken the key himself.

He got up and checked to be sure his gun was loaded, then went out of the office and locked the door behind him. He had wondered why Rainie hadn't been to town lately and whenever he had dropped by, she had seemed preoccupied. The reason was now obvious. She must have somehow fallen in with the kidnappers who had Jordan Lane. Since Rainie was a law-abiding citizen, it made sense that she was being held hostage, too. Her letting the kidnappers use her typewriter could have been a way of alerting someone to where they were.

For a minute Tom considered going after the FBI men and telling them what he had figured out, but he decided against it. If the kidnappers were hiding at Rainie's house they would be accustomed to seeing Tom's car drive up. With luck Tom might be able to capture them before they realized he knew they were there.

Besides, he didn't like the way the FBI men had treated him. They might be hotshot G-men, but he was every bit as good a law enforcement officer as they were. Besides, Lupine was his town, and he'd take care of his own.

Bratcher and his cohorts walked down Lupine's narrow sidewalk to the post office, which was easily identified by the American flag out front. Sandwiched into what had once been an alley dividing the grocery and general store, the post office was small and narrow, with its few postal boxes on one side and a bulletin board with wanted posters on the other. A middle-aged man stood behind a barred window sorting the mail. When the strangers entered, he grinned and said, "Hi. Can I do something for you?"

Once again Bratcher produced the ransom note and envelope. "FBI. Do you remember processing this envelope?"

The man frowned down at it. "Hang on a minute." He looked toward the back of the office. "Jack? You still here?"

"Yo!"

Bratcher glanced at his men and rolled his eyes upward. They sighed in unison.

Jack sauntered up the length of the room, past the pigeon holes for sorting mail and the canvas bags used to transport it. "Yep?"

Ed handed him the paper. "Do you recollect seeing this envelope before? It rings a bell with me, but I can't quite figure it out."

"Sure I do. Picked it up out to Rainie's place a few days ago." He frowned through the bars at the three men. "What're you fellers doing with Rainie's mail?"

"Read it," Ed said. "Looks like a ransom note."

"I'll take that back now," Bratcher said abruptly.

Jack snorted. "There's somebody pulling your leg. Rainie ain't kidnapped nobody."

Bratcher took the paper and returned it to his pocket. "Who is this Rainie and how do we get there?"

THE TWO WEEKS since she had seen Lucas had been an eternity. Countless times she had considered going to his cabin to find out whether he was all right, but her promise kept her away. She had slept only fitfully, and had been so preoccupied with concern about Lucas's welfare and trying to figure some way to get him out of this dilemma, her work had gone by the wayside. Finally she had concluded running to Mexico wouldn't be the answer. In the first place, she wasn't sure they could make it without being caught. In the second, she and Lucas were both too basically honest to be able to live happily as fugitives.

She had heard about plea bargaining, in which accomplices to crimes were often given suspended sentences in return for their incriminating testimony. Up until now she had been against this practice. Lucas would, of course, know the names of all the people who were involved, and with his help the police could bring them all to justice. She wasn't too sure how a person went about setting up a plea bargain, but she was sure Tom must know. All she had to do was to take Lucas to Tom.

A knock on her back door gave her a start. She wasn't expecting anyone. Almost afraid to hope, she ran to answer it. "Lucas!"

She threw herself into his embrace and felt his arms close about her. He was back, and he was safe. "I was so worried about you," she said, his chest muffling her words.

"You were?" He hugged her tight, then drew back enough to kiss her. "Lord, but I've missed you." He kissed her again, this time more deeply.

"Are you sure you're okay?" she asked when their lips parted.

"Of course I am," he said with a laugh.

"Great. I've got it all figured out. We have to go to Tom Hanford, and you can tell him everything."

"What?" Lucas grinned down at her. "What are you talking about?"

"Jordan Lane, of course. The kidnapping!"

"You mailed that letter to Aaron Tavish, didn't you?"

"Yes, but I wish I hadn't. It's been on the news, and . . ."

"What's been on the news? Rainie, I don't understand any of this."

"Look, I know you must have been pressured into this—blackmailed, maybe—but we'll work around that. Tom is my friend, and once we explain everything—"

She broke off as the sheriff's car wheeled into her driveway and came to a screeching halt. Tom Hanford got out, his face wary and his hand resting on the handle of his revolver. "Tom?" she said in surprise from the doorway.

"Move easy, Rainie," Tom said. "Just move away slow."

"Tom, what on earth are you talking about?" she demanded.

Lucas took a step forward as if to put his body between the sheriff and Rainie.

"Hold it! Right there!" Tom had the pistol out of his holster and pointed at Lucas before Rainie could blink. Bracing it in both hands, Tom said, "Get away from him, Rainie! He can't hurt you now."

"Are you crazy?" she gasped.

"You have the right to remain silent," Tom said, not taking his eyes off Lucas. "You have the right—"

"You're arresting me!" Lucas exclaimed. "Who the hell is this, Rainie?"

"It's just Tom." Rainie stalked toward the sheriff. "What do you think you're doing?"

All at once a black car skidded around the corner of her house, throwing clots of grass from under its wheels. Three men in dark suits piled out and leaped into position, using the car as a shield. All three guns were pointed at Rainie.

She fell back a step.

"Freeze!" Bratcher yelled. "FBI! Hold it right there, ma'am! I'm arresting you for the kidnapping of Jordan Lane. You have the right to remain silent. You have—"

"What?" Tom cried out. "Are you boys plain crazy? *He's* the kidnapper. This is Rainie Sheenan."

Lucas moved forward slowly, his hands well in sight and away from his body. "If you'll all just calm down, I think I can explain everything."

"Oh, Lucas," Rainie sobbed. "It's too late to plea bargain now."

Lucas turned back to the men. "I'm Lucas Dalton." He looked at Rainie. "I'm also Jordan Lane." Her mouth dropped open in amazement. "Jordan Lane is my pen name. Nobody has kidnapped me. I've been living in my cabin up the mountain while I write a book."

The FBI men glanced at each other. "We have a warrant for the arrest of Rainie Sheenan for your kidnapping."

Tom glared at them. "Now how in the hell did you get a warrant between coming in my office and getting out here? They're lying, Rainie."

"Look," Lucas said, "there hasn't been any kidnapping at all. I'm right here. There's my horse. If you look in the slicker tied to the saddle, you'll find the manuscript I just finished."

Bratcher jerked his head toward the horse and one of the silent men holstered his gun and went to look.

After a hesitation, Tom lowered his gun and said, "You're the man Rainie said she's been seeing?"

"That's right." Lucas looked at Rainie, who appeared to be in shock. "I had planned to tell you in a less dramatic way."

"You're Jordan Lane?" she gasped. "*The* Jordan Lane?"

He nodded.

"You're *not* a kidnapper?"

He cocked his head to one side, and squinted at her in puzzlement. "You thought I was a kidnapper? And you let me... Rainie!"

She blushed.

"Here it is," the man at the horse called. "It's addressed to Aaron Tavish and is from Lucas Dalton."

Rainie glared back at him accusingly. "You might have told me!"

Bratcher looked uncertainly at Lucas. "You do fit the description of Dalton. I assume you have some identification?"

Lucas produced his wallet and showed the man his driver's license. "Satisfied?"

"Does that mean you don't want her arrested?"

"No, thanks. I'd rather marry her." Lucas grinned at Rainie. "Well? Which would you prefer?"

Her mouth had dropped open. "You want to marry me? What about all you said about not wanting any commitments?"

"I changed my mind. Did you?"

She nodded slowly. "I'm not afraid of commitments. Not when they're with you."

"Does that mean yes?" He slowly walked toward her.

"Yes. It means yes." She came to meet him.

Tom looked at Bratcher and smiled. "Looks like none of us gets to arrest anybody."

Bratcher glared at him.

Lucas put his arms around Rainie. "Will you object to also marrying Jordan Lane?"

"I can't think of any two men I'd rather marry." She lifted her face for his kiss.

HARLEQUIN
Temptation

COMING NEXT MONTH

#293 THE ADENTURER Jayne Ann Krentz (Ladies and Legends, Book 2)

When romance writer Sarah Fleetwood hired ex-adventurer Gideon Trace to help her locate an old family heirloom, she got more than she bargained for. Gideon was the image of the hero she'd depicted in so many of her books—mysterious, dangerously appealing . . . but unavailable. Sarah had to figure out what made him tick—or forego the happy ending. . . .

#294 ONLY HUMAN Kelly Street

Librarian Caitlin Stewart was just getting over her painful past when Lee Michaels charged through her carefully placed blocks. His investigation into football recruitment violations pointed to Caitlin's late husband. Lee would need all the right moves for the most important play of his life—getting Caitlin to love him.

#295 RIPE FOR THE PICKING Mary Tate Engels

When wounded law-enforcement officer Brett Meyer returned to his father's New Mexico ranch, he received a hero's welcome—from everyone except Annie Clayton. Annie found his presence unsettling. Her life was firmly rooted in her struggling apple farm and Brett was restless to move on. Annie feared he'd leave again . . . and take her heart with him.

#296 GUARDED MOMENTS JoAnn Ross

Chantal Giraudeau was a princess—and she expected everyone to treat her royally. But special agent Caine O'Bannion wasn't about to indulge her every whim. His assignment was to guard her during her American tour. And protect her, he would . . . even if it meant keeping watch over her day and night!

The Adventurer

JAYNE ANN KRENTZ

Remember THE PIRATE (Temptation #287), the first book of
Jayne Ann Krentz's exciting trilogy Ladies and Legends? Next
month Jayne brings us another powerful romance, THE
ADVENTURER (Temptation #293), in which Kate, Sarah and
Margaret — three long-time friends featured in THE PIRATE
— meet again.

A contemporary version of a great romantic myth, THE
ADVENTURER tells of Sarah Fleetwood's search for long-
lost treasure and for love. Only when she meets her modern-
day knight-errant Gideon Trace will Sarah know she's found
the path to fortune and eternal bliss....

THE ADVENTURER — available in April 1990! And in June,
look for THE COWBOY (Temptation #302), the third book of
this enthralling trilogy.

**In April, Harlequin brings you the
world's most popular romance author**

JANET DAILEY

No Quarter Asked

Out of print since 1974!

After the tragic death of her father, Stacy's world is shattered. She needs to get away by herself to sort things out. She leaves behind her boyfriend, Carter Price, who wants to marry her. However, as soon as she arrives at her rented cabin in Texas, Cord Harris, owner of a large ranch, seems determined to get her to leave. When Stacy has a fall and is injured, Cord reluctantly takes her to his own ranch. Unknown to Stacy, Carter's father has written to Cord and asked him to keep an eye on Stacy and try to convince her to return home. After a few weeks there, in spite of Cord's hateful treatment that involves her working as a ranch hand and the return of Lydia, his ex-fiancée, by the time Carter comes to escort her back, Stacy knows that she is in love with Cord and doesn't want to go.

**Watch for *Fiesta San Antonio* in July and
For Bitter or Worse in September.**

JDA-1